MOTIVE FOR A KILL

John Newton Chance

Chivers Press
Bath, England

G.K. Hall & Co.
Thorndike, Maine USA

This Large Print edition is published by Chivers Press, England, and by G.K. Hall & Co., USA.

Published in 1997 in the U.K. by arrangement with Robert Hale Ltd.

Published in 1997 in the U.S. by arrangement with Robert Hale Ltd.

U.K. Hardcover ISBN 0–7451–8952–0 (Chivers Large Print)
U.S. Softcover ISBN 0–7838–1995–1 (Nightingale Collection Edition)

The text of this Large Print edition is unabridged.
Other aspects of the book may vary from the original edition.

Set in 16 pt. New Times Roman.

Printed in Great Britain on acid-free paper.

British Library Cataloguing in Publication Data available

Library of Congress Cataloging-in-Publication Data

Chance, John Newton.
Motive for a kill / by John Newton Chance.
p. cm.
ISBN 0–7838–1995–1 (lg. print : sc)
1. Large type books. I. Title.
[PR6005.H28M68 1997]
823′.912—dc20 96–35471

CHAPTER ONE

1

I think the trouble about women is that you feel more strongly when you leave them than when you're with them. Absence does not make the heart grow fonder, but only that it's got something missing.

I do not know what Freddie Lawrence had that all the other girls somehow hadn't, and I spent a great deal of time thinking about it, trying to find out.

Then, without admitting it, I spent some time trying to think of a simple excuse for going down to Tregarrok; one that she wouldn't see through.

Now and again I surfaced and wondered what sort of age I was, twisting myself in such a puerile manner.

I was, that spring, at home in Cornwall, which is not forty miles from Tregarrok, and I did think that dropping in accidentally at the farm might be a reasonable approach, but I was too conscious of its possible importance, and hesitated.

Then my partner, John Marsh, rang up on the morning of May fourteenth.

'An old friend of yours is approaching the Cornish peninsula,' he said, 'after an absence of a few months—far too few.'

'Bad news?'
'I don't know that, but it's important. That business at Tregarrok; a sort of slaughterhouse which you walked into.'
'I'm not likely to forget it. So?'
'One of the main conspirators—the agent, Congle. Remember him?'
'A breathless villain. Of course I remember! What are you getting at?'
'He got off on appeal yesterday.'
'Did he? How on earth did he fix that?'
'A legal fault in the summing-up of his case. He was done as an accomplice, you recall. A difficult man to get a fix on.'
'Difficult to hold, too, by the sound of it. Haven't the police got other charges?'
'I have the wire they're just going to let him go. You remember they never found the connection—the organisation the Congle outfit did business with.'
'Such a firm wouldn't go back there,' I said.
'It offers many advantages, Jonathan. Loneliness. Sea routes. Very quiet roads and tracks.'
'You're thinking of smuggling. But the Tregarrok outfit was a gang of jumpers. They offered an escape route to successful bank robbers, then murdered the robbers and took the loot. They had no reason to smuggle. They were doing all right as they were.'
'Well, it's thought interest is still on that house and the police want to leave it to start up

again and really get going without interference. They want the naughties to hang themselves, but they want somebody there to watch it out and give them the wire when it's ripe for the raid.'

'That's a nice little number for some incipient suicide.'

'Now, the interesting part is—'

'I don't like the lead-in. Me, do you mean?'

'Well now, you have this girl there, pretend. After all, she was pretty good, wasn't she?'

'She's a cross-eyed rake,' I said, and it hurt. 'I only consorted in the name of the game.'

'If that was a cross-eyed rake I saw in the witness box, buy me one.'

'Each to his own gout, as the French say. What have you been cooking with the coppers? I don't like this.'

'It's just they want an experienced eye to note what goes on, and you have the password—this girl Freda Lawrence.'

'But I can't just walk in and give her some flowers. She grows them.'

'Oh, come off it, Jonathan. Look at it this way; if you don't agree to hang around and what the coppers suspect does happen, she'll get trouble, and she might not get out of it.'

Now, I remembered very well that she had been in the middle of serious trouble before, when Congle was operating at the empty house, and nothing would have shifted her from her farm.

'She wouldn't leave there,' I said. 'She's strong-minded. Obstinate. Stupid.'

'Very sensible. We don't want her to leave it. That would make the operators wonder what was going on.'

'Yes, I realise that. Look, why don't you get an eye who knows about farming, then he could get taken on as a temporary hand.'

'That's an idea,' he said thoughtfully.

'On the other hand, he couldn't stay there all night,' I said.

'But you could,' he said.

'I didn't say that. I said nobody could stay there all night.'

'Oh, come off it. Where's your professional skill? You're supposed to be able to insinuate yourself by charm and expertise—'

'Are you being insulting?'

'Heavens above, man! What's the matter with you?'

'Nothing. What have you really got in mind? What have you cooked, you ragbag?'

'Visit your old friend. Help her. Pretend to fall and come and come again. You know the action, man. It might hurt, if she's the susceptible kind, but better a broken heart than a broken neck, Jonathan. I quote Doctor Johnson.'

'You're a bloody fool. She isn't the kind of girl to fall for that sort of ploy.'

'Well, go for the straight sex. She's probably fond of bulls.'

'I find you somewhat offensive, John.'
He paused.
'You're not suggesting you have a thing for this girl, are you?' he said slowly.
'I didn't suggest anything. No.'
'Then why so sensitive?'
'I am not sensitive. I just don't think you realise the sort of girl she is. She is very difficult. Bloody minded. If a man walked in as you suggest—either way you suggest—he'd be bounced out on his ear. It's like that.'
'Well look, dear boy, think on it and get going. You know her so you'll see the best way to approach the matter—but it's essential you get to that Tregarrok place and stick there until you get wind of the action.'
'And how do I signal the action from that place? If I'm watching, you can bet somebody will take interest and watch me.'
'Use your RS9 and every other little thing that will deafen them.'
'Will the police have the RS9?'
'They will.'
'And how far will they be from me?'
'Five miles.'
'That's a long way on those roads. They're only single track, mostly. Easily blocked.'
'They'll be in a cottage at Lower Pendell, and the vehicles will be parked round the village, unmarked. You know the game.'
'I know the game when the place is easily get-at-able, but Tregarrok has never been

opened up. One tractor on its side and you've stopped the lot for quite a while, and that might be important—for me.'

'Then think of it all as saving the girl. Knight Errant stuff. After all, you're in the Round Table country. Fall in with the legendary armour.'

'There is a point, John, which you've skated over. I have been there before. If Congle sees me, he'll guess what I'm at.'

'My dear Jonathan, this is what I have been trying to make clear to you. You are smitten with the girl, and having a vacation, what's more natural than you should hang around?'

'You make it sound easy, and it's not. People in the villages round saw me, and they must have connected me with the great event at Tregarrok when the gang burst.'

'Any man's entitled to go a-hunting.'

I thought about it.

'Why do you think the main operators would go back there and take a risk of the place still being watched? Missing loot?'

'You know most of the banks had deposit boxes stolen, and it was impossible to assess what was in a lot of them. Some people are shy.'

'I know that. But if the banks don't know, how do the crooks?'

'I have a surprise I was saving till the end.'

'Well?'

'Last week an unexploded German mine was

found in the mud of the Thames Estuary.'

'What are you waiting for? I don't want to buy it.'

'The Navy boys blew it up in the proper manner, but the tremors disturbed a body which had been lying on the river bed full of holes and with concrete attached by a chain. The body got free because the flesh had rotted off and the anklet couldn't hold the bones.'

'That's bloody gruesome. So there's a gang murder. I'll buy it. Anybody we know?'

'A man identified—after some trouble—as Isaac Kraw, a diamond importer and fence. Photos were obtained after visits to his legal home, and three banks identified him as a deposit box customer in the names Eli, Lowson and Jacobson, one name to each bank.

'Two of those banks were robbed and deposit boxes taken, belonging to Jacobson and Eli.'

'He was a big fence?'

'It seems, from documents at his own home and other properties that he had a turnover of three to four million a year.'

'Why, that's a turnover! International operator?'

'He had to be, at that price.'

'Were there signs that somebody had tried to ask him where his money box was?'

'Plenty. A lot of torture. I think they had to shoot him in the end.'

'And you think the gang that killed him will

be coming down in the end.'

'I think they were there before, but what they didn't know was that Kraw's boxes were stolen. He was in the water four months.'

'And how was it they suddenly found the numbers of the stolen boxes, because it's a dead cert Kraw didn't report anything stolen.'

'Of course he didn't. The banks couldn't get in touch because Lowson, Jacobson and Eli didn't exist, nor did their addresses. That was a dead end for the police, but their main interest was to get the bank robbers.'

'You know, John, this doesn't sound like the original gangs' descendants panning Kraw. It's somebody muscling in.'

'Possibly. But you'll find out. As you said, Kraw was international and I think, so is this lot.'

'John, this isn't our sort of work. You know that.'

'Normally no. I admit that, but the police are badly in need of preventive action, and you can provide it.'

He waited for me to say something, but I didn't.

'All right. Doubtful,' he said. 'Think about it. Ring me back tonight.'

'About what?'

'About the way you're going to do it.'

He rang off before my retort got to him, so it was almost as if the obscenity came back into my own ear.

2

Without any external feelings, I would have gone back to Tregarrok just to get the best of the situation. Without the sordid criminal challenge, I would, in the end, have gone back there anyway. But the two were together and I spent the rest of that day thinking the situation from two distinct angles, one personal, the other impersonal.

Of course, I realised that both were the same as far as my personal comfort were to be concerned, but on the time scale so different. One might be the beginning of a good life and the other the end of it.

The odd part was I wanted to go back on both counts of personal endeavour, but didn't want them mixed, but it seemed that it would be impossible to separate them.

The fact now was that I couldn't go back and see her at all without taking on the job, and I couldn't take over the job and not see her.

I spent a while thinking women were a bloody nuisance and then an idea occurred.

I had gone to Tregarrok as a surveyor of the house acting for an invisible purchaser. As far as I knew, that act had never been blown. It had been agreed that throughout the proceedings in court and in connection with that institution, my own occupation had not been revealed.

The main reason being that I had gone to that damned—and I mean that in the correct sense—place on behalf of an institution generally understood to be the Secret Service.

Throughout all the vicissitudes of my later life I have always kept my association with the body of surveyors which I joined when starting in my professional career, and have not willingly done anything which could have busted that relationship, though I do not practise anymore.

Somewhere in the back of my mind I have always had the intention of going back to it, and perhaps, all being well—myself particularly—I will. The visit to Tregarrok originally was exceptional in that we could think of no other way to examine the place without being shot.

It looked as though, once again, that might be the best way of doing things.

I rang John.

He said, 'Well?'

I said, 'I've not decided. I want to know if the surveyor front was leaked. Make sure from the police and let me know. Otherwise it's off.'

I put the phone down, but I knew it couldn't be off. There was Freddie and she added up to too much.

Just to make sure, that afternoon, of my certainty about Freddie I rang the girl I had been particularly fond of with the object of spending the evening.

'Jonathan?' she said. 'Which Jonathan? Do you mean the one that's nine feet high?'

Well, that wasn't any good. I am not nine feet, but six feet two, and when the girl is a foot less, I suppose it shows. But if nothing else shows either, forget her.

So I went for a walk with the farmer's dog. Whenever I go for a walk the farmer's dog seems to know and very soon, there he is, a golden retriever who spends his time lying around till I go for a walk. But I am being unfair to him. I am not at home that often.

We went away from the house and across the field I use as a landing strip and on beyond into the woods. Roger chased things and sniffed things and watered trees and dug up here and there.

Then suddenly he went 'Wuff!' in a deep throated, warning sort of noise and belted off through the trees leaving the young bright green shoots shivering behind him.

He didn't go far but stopped and woofed and a man came out from behind a tree and stood there quite still so the dog wouldn't go for him.

I called Roger away but he stood there till I came up.

The man said, 'It's all right. I'm trespassing, I 'spect. Sorry.'

I got the dog by the collar and the man turned and tramped away through the woods towards the lane. I told the dog to lay off and stood still watching the man's back.

I was sure I had seen him before, walking away just like that, and for a moment could not think where, nor why I should feel it was important to remember.

Then I placed him. He had been working on Congle's farm eight months before, when I had been involved in the Tregarrok business.

The shock was quite acute, and I wondered first whether Tregarrok, being on my mind, was playing around suggesting things, but I felt too sure. I had seen him there.

And the man had been behind the tree and, without the dog, would have stayed unseen. People trespassing sometimes do such things but that knowledge didn't overbalance my uneasiness over the man being there.

I had been to Congle's farm only once and then for an hour and no more. All that time I had been fully engaged with the curious behaviour of the Congles and their cowman, but I was sure then that I had seen this man walking away across that dirty, unkempt farmyard.

As I stood there trying to make up my mind I heard a motor start and go away.

I turned and went back. The dog left me, as usual, when we passed the farm entrance.

I rang John at his flat, for it was then evening.

'This isn't going to work,' I said. 'One of Congle's men has been here watching for me.'

'What does that matter?' he said. 'You're still a surveyor, and we've fixed a real client for you. A live one this time.'

'I'm being murdered,' I said.

'You get used to it, after a while. The surveyor line wasn't leaked. I've checked everything. You're watertight.'

'And there was this man . . .' I said pointedly.

'Well, so there was this man. Can't surveyors live in plush estates down your end of the bloody country?'

As far as I knew, nobody in my home neighourhood knew what I did when I was away from there.

He waited a bit, then said, 'Yes?'

I said, 'All right. Yes.'

John's description of the suspected situation that could arise at Tregarrok had been quite clear. Previous events he had told made it reasonably certain that any gangsters who turned up at that house would be in a hurry and would not care to have anybody in the way.

Knowing the layout of the place as I did, I couldn't quite see how my surveyor guise could hold up against such people. Previously the main characters concerned at Tregarrok had been local, wearing innocent faces for years and hence not quite so vicious as they might have been.

A gang who had shot a fence full of holes after torture and then sunk him with a concrete block for company was likely to do the same again.

Especially if they thought I knew anything.

Thinking it over it did seem that the 'safest'

pose was that of a surveyor with a right to be there, but more intent on seducing the maiden than on his work.

As I got some things together—things of a personal nature, like my Smith and Wesson .38 and the RS9 pocket radio communicator, a bug detector and other protective devices—my housekeeper packed some clothes.

Mrs Herriot was a widow but entertaining a local policeman with some serious intent. He was a sergeant and senior member of the county force, so before I left I spoke to her.

'I found a trespasser in the wood yesterday. If you see anyone lurking around you don't like, tell the sergeant, or if it's urgent, the farmer. He'll stand by till the sergeant gets here.'

'My, you sound serious,' she said, and smiled. 'I don't mind trespassers. My son is coming over for two days, so I'll be well protected.'

That seemed all right, just in case the lurcher came back again when I had gone, but I doubted he would. I thought he had come just to see if I was there.

I drove to the little town where Congle's office had been, and wondered if it had been shut or opened up by somebody else.

When I walked down the narrow cobbled alley and pushed the brown and paint cracked door I went straight into the Dickensian outer office.

A young man was there in a suit and a high white collar that made his neck look like a post for the ball of his head.

'Mr Congle?' I said, as if I had not heard of Congle's travails.

'Mr Congle is away just now,' the man said, watching me. 'I'm his assistant, James Haigh.'

I explained the purpose of my call.

'I was at Tregarrok before, but that was for a possible private sale which didn't come off. My visit now is different. The house is being considered for classification in the historic buildings category, which will, of course, preserve it. I am acting for the Ministry.'

'Oh, I see,' he said.

It was, of course, a wonderful line, because there could be no possible excuse for trying to refuse permission to get in there and make the survey.

I felt that any other reason I could have given would have met with refusal.

'I haven't heard of this proposal,' he said.

'I heard by phone this morning. They want my opinion on the general state of the place as soon as possible to get it on the list for grants before the programme gets full up.'

'Yes, I see.'

'I should imagine the owner will be pleased. It takes such a financial load off, doesn't it?'

He played it coolly but I could see he was uneasy.

'I wish Mr Congle was here,' he said.

'However, you had better have the keys and I will let him know as soon as I can.'

He opened the door of Congle's office and went in quickly, closing the door again. The fanning action of the door blew out the unmistakeable stink of Congle's own hand-rolled cigarettes.

I half turned and stood so that I looked out of the window but would also see into the office when the door opened.

There was no sound of voices from inside, and two or three minutes passed before the door opened again. Haigh came out and as his body cleared the door behind him I caught a glimpse of untidy, ungainly Congle sitting at the desk. It was only a flash before the door shut, but it was enough to know I hadn't made a mistake.

'Would you sign for these?' the man said, handing me a bunch of keys and putting a scrap of paper on the desk.

I signed, took the keys and left with more to think about on my way to the grim pile on the cliffs.

But as I drove along the narrow, winding lane towards Tregarrok my thought turned entirely towards the girl.

There was no doubt she would be in danger if another set of gangland murderers turned up at the great house. Her farm butted on to the Tregarrok grounds only fifty yards from the house. Her cattle often strayed and broke through the fence and she had to go in and get them back.

If she did that at an inconvenient time and saw something even more inconvenient anything could happen.

I decided to go to the farm first. In any case, it would be in with the part I was going to follow, and not so much of a part at that, so I didn't expect difficulty in the acting.

The farm gate was open to the track cutting across the field to the farmhouse. There were no cattle in the field and nobody seemed to be about at all. Everything was quiet, even deserted, which, on a fine May day, was odd.

I began to feel anxiety at the oddness.

When I stopped under the trees fronting the house and turned off the engine I could hear nothing but the murmur of a quiet sea on the beach below the cliffs.

I got out and went to the door, which was open.

I knocked, but the place was silent and nothing stirred. She had two dogs always about the house or with her, but there was no sign of them.

Some way off I heard a sudden cluck of chickens followed by piggy noises from the sties on the other side of the house.

I went round there, hoping human agency had caused the commotion, but there were only pigs and chickens. I went back to the front of the house and stopped there, looking out over the empty farmland.

Then I looked towards the great house, like the hulk of an old ship, lowering and black under the bright sky.

Tregarrok, as evil as ever. I am not normally superstitious, but that damned place can make anybody feel bad.

I thought I saw somebody moving by the corner of the hulk, but it could have been the shadow of a cloud racing by.

CHAPTER TWO

1

I looked around the deserted landscape and felt an uneasiness bordering on alarm. Though I could see no sign of life about the great house a quarter mile away, it was big enough to hide a hundred if a hundred felt that shy.

Once more I called into the house and again nothing happened. I went into the hall and through to the big kitchen. There was no sign that anything had been left hastily or a sudden departure had taken place.

It looked more as if the place had been abandoned in an orderly manner, though all the household stuff was still there.

Outside I realised I had forgotten the pigs and chickens. Of course they wouldn't have been abandoned willingly.

That made me look at the big house again,

looming black and evil against the blue May sky. It was strange that the place would remain so dark on such a day, but it seemed to have been built by men of the night and had kept its looks.

All the old feeling of apprehension came back to me as I stood there wondering where Freddie was.

Then at the distant field gate I saw a girl on a horse riding slowly towards the farmhouse. She seemed to be looking down at the horse's neck in deep thought. I felt I could not mistake the rough old jeans, the open shirt, the frayed raffia hat and golden hair.

I stood where I was at the corner of the house watching her. She did not look up at all. She might almost have been asleep as the horse went his own way towards the stable and cowsheds further on.

I went down towards her. The horse halted with its back to me. I shouted.

'Freddie! Ahoy!'

The girl sat up straight and then turned her head and shoulders.

'Who the hell are you?' she said.

* * *

That morning, at our offices in Surrey, John Marsh had a caller, a man named Zeiss. He was a quiet, restless fellow who chain smoked all the time, but smoked each cigarette only half way down. He marched around the office as if trying to see out of all the windows at once.

'Why do you think somebody would follow you here?' asked John.

The man swung round sharply.

'I din say that!' he snapped.

'You acted it. You think you've been followed. Right. So you're an informer and you've come here to inform . . . on what?'

He lit another cigarette though the one he was smoking was only just lit. He ground it out in an ashtray.

'I know about Ikey Kraw,' he said. 'I want enough to get out of here.'

John sat back and looked at him.

'Ikey Kraw?' he said, as if he didn't know the name.

'You know about him,' Zeiss said. 'He was in glass and ended up in the water business.'

'You mean he was drowned?'

'He had some lead in him first, for weighting,' said Zeiss, moving about almost like an eccentric dancer in his agitation.

'All right. So this is about a man who was murdered and thrown in the river,' said John. 'He was in diamonds. But you're in the wrong shop. You want the police.'

'I wouldn't dare go near a police shop.'

'All right. But what made you think of coming here? We don't buy police business.'

'Look, I've got a friend in the Squad. I've done a lot of small business with him in times back. He said if things got hot and I needed to quit to get on to you.'

'When did he say it?'

'He kept shoving me. About Ikey. He knew I knew but I didn't want the chop so I shut down and I kept shut down. But the time's running short. I need to get out now. Things are moving too fast.'

'What man in the Squad?'

'Detective Inspector Fennick.'

John knew Fennick, but did not say so.

'And this man Kraw. You say he was a diamond thief?'

'No, no, no. He was in the business, and he fenced as a safe line, but always glass, never anything else. Big fellow on the straight and under it. Thing about Ikey was he was so big out in front, not many suspected he was in the back door business as well, you see. Highly respected.'

'And he ended up in the water,' said John. 'Perhaps I read all that in the papers. What else is there?'

'I need enough to get out.'

'I'll have to see if the information is worth that price.'

The visitor lit yet another cigarette. The office was becoming littered with his half burnt refuse.

'I'll trust you,' he said at last.

'Then get on with it.'

'All the fenced stuff was in a safe deposit,

spread out in several banks.'

'We know that.'

'Some of the boxes had nothing but sand in them.'

'Sand?' John sat up.

'It was the mislead, see, in case any of the gangs got on to the deposit boxes, he faked some so when the boys stole the ticket and went and got the box there was nothing but bloody sand. Ikey would have the signal when the ticket was nicked and get his bodyguard in action. You see?'

'Yeah. But supposing they drew a genuine box?'

'The tickets for those was held by another man, an agent who had all the deeds of his property. Feller called Strange, got an office in Bath. That's the bit that's worth the money. Without me there's no link between Ikey and Strange, you see?'

'I see. Yes, I see. But it's some time since Ikey was done in. Why do you suddenly want to cash and carry?'

'Because I've had enough and they're taking too much interest now for me.'

'They're beating after that private fortune of Ikey's?'

He put out his cigarette and did not light another. He pointed at John.

'You've got a man called Blake.'

'I have a partner called Blake.'

'Well, this mob think Mr Blake knows where

the stuff is.'

John already suspected that, so had I. It was the reason why I had gone to Tregarrok.

'Do they know where Mr Blake is?' said John, as if it didn't matter that much.

'No. No, they don't know where he is. But they think I do. Get it, mister? I want out before they get to asking me any questions.'

'Right. Just one question. What sort of agent is this man Strange?'

'Supposed to be a land agent—estate, you know. I wouldn't be sure of anybody's real trade when Ikey chose them.'

'Right.' John got up. 'I'll see you clear. There's a security van calling in ten minutes. They'll lend you a uniform. You go in that. Where are you going? What sort of money?'

'Brittany. I'll get down to Cherbourg and get a boat. Doesn't matter where so long as it's not here. I'd better have dollars.'

2

'I thought you were Freddie,' I said.

'I'm her sister, Laura. Who are you?'

I introduced myself as the surveyor who had been here before.

'Then she's still here?' I ended up.

'She drove the herd over to the old farm this morning.' She dismounted without help from me and looked as if she didn't want any. 'She didn't say anything about a surveyor coming.'

'I'm doing the house over there, but we met

when I was here the last time, and I thought a neighbourly call was in order.'

She looked at me very quietly, but said a lot without saying a word.

'Ah,' she sighed at the end, and began to unsaddle the pony.

She was a difficult girl to make conversation with.

'I don't know when she's coming back,' she said, hoisting the saddle on to her shoulder. 'Could be any time.'

She took the saddle into the shed then came out again.

'Still here?' she said, as if it didn't matter.

'Still,' I said.

'Insufferable pod,' she said, and freed the horse from the rest of his trappings. 'Go on—feed. Roam.'

She smacked the pony's rump and the animal cantered away across the field. She then turned to me. I was uncertain as to whether her remark had been meant for me or the horse. She then treated me as the horse and lightly smacked my rump.

'Come in,' she said, and walked towards the house.

'I came to see Freddie,' I said.

'Okay. So you did. Come on in. I want to talk, but not out here.'

So I followed her into the house and the kitchen.

'Sit,' she said and pointed to a chair.

'Thank you,' I said ironically, and sat.

She then sat on me, put one arm round my neck and took my right hand and put it inside her shirt, then settled herself against me.

'Do you fish?' she said.

'For what?' I said.

'Fish,' she said. 'I've got a boat but I can't fish. If you fish, okay.'

It was okay by any standards as one way of passing an hour or two. She was as desirable as I had found her sister, but a degree or two barmier.

'Are you staying here, then?' I said.

She wriggled a bit and said, 'Why? Am I heavy?'

'No. I meant staying in the house.'

'Oh yes. Holiday. So I won this boat, you see and brought it here but it's stuck in a gate.'

'That doesn't sound like very good navigation.'

She sighed.

'It's on a big trailer, clot. The man I won the boat from brought it down here, but he got it stuck in this gate and had to get back in a hurry, so he went. That was Tuesday.'

'It's been there since Tuesday?'

'We've been waiting for the man to mend the tractor, but he hasn't come yet. Would you like to survey the ship and see what you think?'

'Where is it?'

'In next door's gate.'

'The big house?'

'Yes.'
'How did it get there?'
'We passed the farm by mistake and went on there, and Toby thought he could turn round there, but he couldn't.'
'Then he conveniently went.'
'I didn't want him to stay unless he won the boat back.'
'He must be pretty well off to play with yachts for stakes.'
'He makes a bomb,' she said. 'He's with a diamond firm, you see, and they can always make a little more on the side. It's part of the perks.'
Diamonds seemed to be cropping up too frequently.
'What firm?'
'Well, it's Kraw in Hatton Garden, but the man disappeared a few weeks ago, so Toby's in charge at the moment.'
Oh no, I thought. This is going to be very complicated.

3

We got into my car. I turned it round and headed for the gate again.
'You can tow anything with this, can't you?' she said.
'I don't know about battleships,' I said. 'This boat of yours sounds as if it's getting on that way. Do you know Toby very well?'
'It was a party. A real slosh up. Money

galore. Buckets of booze, barrels of caviare, cheques like confetti, because we played cards and roulette and chemmy and poker, and I was playing with this Toby.

'Well, I lost all my money to him and my clothes as well, you see, so then he said "Right; let's go to bed", and I said "No," and he said "Why not?" and I said "You look funny," and—do you know?—he got raving mad, he was so vain, vain about everything.

'He got so mad he started boasting about his flat and his yacht and all that, and so I said, "Right; let's gamble".

'And he said, "What about? You're skint", so I said, "I bet going to bed, my clothes and your yacht".

'Well he laughed and told me I was the loser and hadn't got these things to bet against. Well, I don't understand all this betting business, so I played it scornful, you might say, and hoity as well, and sniffed and all that ha-ha contemptuous which takes doing when you're sitting there in nothing but a dry Martini, but it got him all riled.

'He bet the bed part and lost. Then I pushed him on to the clothes and won them back, and he was getting so mad he'd have bet his mother-in-law—no, perhaps not her—but you know what I mean.'

I saw very well what she meant.

'And you won them all?'

'Yes. So he had to offer to drag it down here

for me, and he did that very easily. I was surprised the way he agreed because on the night I won he wouldn't. He said I'd have to accept it in the middle of Piccadilly or nowhere. Like that, he was. Short.'

'And next day?' I stopped at the gateway out of the field. We had been trundling slowly to let her talk.

'He rang up and asked where I thought I wanted it, so I told him and he asked where exactly, so I told him that, and he said he'd have to see if he could manage the time.'

'And he rang off?'

'Yes. He rang later and said he would do it next day, that was Tuesday. So he came down. I showed him the way but we went past, and then all like I said.'

'You live in London?'

'I've been trying to. It's very expensive. You know, I really couldn't afford to lose those clothes.'

'And then you thought you'd better come down here, recuperate and sponge off your sister?'

'But of course! What are sisters for?'

'I don't know. I haven't one.'

I drove on to where the great walls of the Tregarrok estate curved in off the narrow road into the iron gates which I had last seen padlocked and chained.

Then one could hardly see the gates because of the big yacht which stood on a four wheeled trailer, its stern shoved right into the gates.

We got out. I walked along to the back. He had made a surprisingly good job of it. The spikes on the gate top, about eight feet high, were stuck through the stern of the hull.

'An amateur can't do this,' I said. 'You need a boat builder who knows how to do it without causing any more damage.'

'Oh dear,' she said.

I went underneath the damage and saw that the spikes which had been driven into the structure were still there stuck inside. They hadn't snapped off.

'Furthermore,' I said, 'either the boat must be lifted or the gates unhinged, and it'll be a job to do that without lifting the boat several inches.'

She looked at it.

'Do you think he did it for spite?' she said.

I went out into the road and looked at it from there. It looked to me that he could have backed the boat in so far in front of the gates, uncoupled then gone down the road, turned the car, come back, coupled up and pulled it round the other way.

Instead of which he had driven the thing backwards as far and as hard as he could go and got it stuck fairly on the top of the gates which, having been locked and chained, hadn't been able to give way more than a few inches.

In fact, it looked deliberate.

'Yes,' I said. 'He might have done it for spite.

There's nothing we can do but send for somebody who knows boats and has the necessary tackle.'

We got back in the car. There was a gateway in view further on in which I turned my large vehicle without trouble.

'You got here in daylight?' I asked.

'Yes. Fairly steamed along. Big Land-Rover it was. He said he hired it, always did when he wanted to heave the boat somewhere.'

Kraw's stand-in, Tregarrok, the robberies, the murder for the hidden loot, the murders which had already happened in this dark house in pursuit of that treasure, all seemed to tie together in an uncomfortable manner.

'When he rang up the first time that morning, did you tell him exactly where it was to go?'

'I think so. When he asked I said, "Down Cornwall" and he said, "That's a hell of a way. Whereabouts there?" Well, then I said. "It's a farm..." and he said, "You want it on a *farm*?" all surprised...'

'And then you told him the address?' I interrupted because I thought all these retailed conversations would go on all the rest of the day if I didn't.

'Yes. Then he said, "Well, I'd better see if I can arrange it," and I said...'

'Did he know the address?'

'Well, he never said so, and he didn't know the way. I suppose he wanted time to see when he could have the Land-Rover and when he could take time off, you see.'

'When he backed the boat to turn round he must have driven it backwards pretty hard?'

'Yes, he did. I shouted, "Hold it—!" but he hit the gates then so it wasn't much good. He grumbled and said I ought to have got out to look.'

We turned in the farm gate.

'Do you think he did it for spite, then?' she said.

'Something like that.'

What he had done, very effectively, was to stop any other vehicle getting into Tregarrok unless noisy and noticeable manpower and machines were first brought to the scene to unblock the gate.

Engaging such labour would bring immediate attention to the hirer from the firm employed, the men used, and the locals who might be about to know of the operation.

If one lot of crooks set out on such a process, then another would very soon know and what was planned as a clear run would become an unwanted fracas.

So Toby had gone to some trouble to block the only vehicle entrance.

It showed that he knew what Tregarrok was and that somebody he didn't like intended to go there.

It also showed that he knew a vehicle was going to be needed for what had to be done.

Which seemed to indicate that Toby knew an awful lot, and much of that lot had to do with the late Kraw's fencing hobby.

In which case Toby, the gambler, was taking a very good chance of gambling himself into being late also.

No one was about when we got back to the farmhouse.

'How long has she been gone over there?' I said.

'I don't know. My watch stopped. She said "why don't you get your watch mended this morning?" and I said, "Well lend me the car", and she said, "I want that", so I said, "How in hell do you park a horse, then?" And she...'

'She drove the cattle in a car?'

'No. It was over there. The car. She went early on in the car and came back with the horse. Then she walked off with the cattle.'

She went to the stove.

'I'll get some tea,' she said. 'Fred won't be long. She said she would go on to Mar. Something she wanted. I remember now.'

'Oh. I see.' The girl's tape recordings of conversations seemed to be able to leave out important details, considering I had been wanting to see Freddie for an hour or more.

'I don't know how she sticks it here,' she said, filling the kettle. 'There's nobody here at all now. When Dad was alive there was always people round of one sort and another, but all there is now is a couple of hired boys. People seem to have got scared off the place or something.'

'Did Freddie say that?'

'Well, she told me about the fry-up next door a few months back, but you'd think it would bring the gawpers down, not scare them off. It doesn't seem natural.'

'Didn't you come down to see what had happened?'

'I was away doing a film.'

'You're in the film business?'

'When I can get in. There's a whole wodge of waiting around. You get some birds who want to do it themselves.'

'I'm sorry?'

'I do the tumble-about stuff. The stunts. I fall off things and that. I was always good at that at home. I had to do a course of it and it frightened me to death. At school the only thing I was good at was gym. I was in a school team and we represented the county once. I broke my nidnod bone and got left out the day before.'

She made the tea.

'Who took you to the gambling party?'

She looked at me sharply.

'That's a funny kind of all-of-a-sudden question.'

'It isn't really. Those parties are hard to get into.'

'Oh, I see what you mean. I went with Percy. He's in our firm. Do anything Perce. He'll dive on his head from the top of the Eiffel Tower for the money. He went for the money. He wanted me to get some attention to take it off him.'

'Did he say why?'

'He said he was going to put one over on them and wanted to do the lead-up at the right moment without people watching him before.'

'What did he do?'

'Well, he got skint. That wasn't hard because he didn't have much to start with. Then he put in a couple of IOUs and lost them, so he stood up, shouted out something dreadful so everybody in the room looked at him—that's routine stuff, of course—then he rushed to the french windows, pulled them open and rushed out on to the balcony and jumped over into the street . . .

'Except, of course, he didn't. He'd got it all worked out. He jumped the balustrade but tripped himself so he went down and tipped himself under with the bottom of it, got hold of the trellis fixed to the wall and hitched himself down gently.

'Then he ran round the house while screams were coming from the window. The balcony filled up. Lots of people ran out and down the stairs.

'While they did that, he ran round the house, in the back, upstairs and cleared the cash like a broom.

'He was so damn quick he took me by surprise. I knew he was going to pull one, but I thought it was just a hoax. I didn't know it was going to be a sweep up like that.

'He was off in no time. Of course, nobody called the police because it wasn't a licensed place, so he'd got it made, our Percy.'

'That was after you'd won your yacht?'

'I wasn't even in the room. I was getting my clothes back on.'

'Quite a performance.'

'Well, it took me, and I know the business. I never thought he'd twist it like that. I'm a bit simple, I suppose.'

I looked past her.

'Who's your friend?' I said.

A man had appeared at the kitchen window, looked in and almost immediately he saw who was there, he turned and started to run towards the gate leading out to the cliff walk.

I went to the window. She stood there staring at the running man.

'It's Percy!' she said.

'Are you sure? Remember you've just had him very much in mind.'

'Well . . .' she said. 'I think so. Why else should he run away when he saw me?'

Or when he saw me, I thought.

CHAPTER THREE

1

In the brief seconds before I ran out of the house in pursuit I saw Percy run straight for the cliff edge. I had seen a man walk over that edge months before. He had died on the rocks a hundred and fifty feet below.

I ran across the kitchen and out of the open front door. As I turned towards the gate to the cliff path I saw the running man go over the edge.

He did not jump, but seemed to run straight on over, then disappear abruptly.

As I ran to the gate and vaulted it, I hoped that the girl's story of the fake leap from the gaming house balcony was being repeated, but it would be difficult here, even for an expert.

At the cliff edge I looked down at the quiet sea swirling about the black, broken teeth of the rocks far below. There was no body.

The cliff face folded in under the edge where I stood, then thrust out again and went down in a series of very steep ragged steps.

I lay down on the edge and looked over and tried to see under and into the recess. I could not.

The girl came running up.

'A mirror,' I said.

She fished a small one out of the pocket of the gaping shirt and gave it to me. I held it out at arm's length and tilted it so that I could see under the cliff top.

There were breaks and holes and bits of torn and forgotten scrub from earlier cliff falls, but no man was there.

I got up.

'Is he—?' she said.

'I think he did that trick again, and there is quite a range of conveniences just below here. He could hide in a crack, or crawl away through one.'

'But how did he find out there were any?' she said sharply.

'That's the point. He was probably told where to look, then all he had to do was check it for himself.'

'How would anybody know? I mean, except coastguards and that.'

'You could spot likely places with powerful glasses from the sea. This was, after all, a great landing place for smugglers and wreckers. It has many handy spots where angels would certainly fear to tread.'

'But Percy, I mean . . . He never seemed that sort! Not a crook . . .'

'Well, if he's an innocent bystander he cooked up that little performance at your gaming club without much hesitation.'

'Yes, but he was hard up. He'd lost money and he'd put out IOUs and some of those people are very vicious when it comes to bets not being paid.'

'Yes, I know. But organised gangs don't take on ordinary debtors and instruct them to help in tricky crimes.'

'What tricky crimes?' She was startled.

'Any crime is tricky if you're going to press amateurs into helping.'

She looked at me with cool, calculating blue eyes.

'You're not really a detective, are you?' she said.

'Everyone is, at some time or other. It depends whether you get paid for it, or not.'

'Oh.' She looked over the cliff again. 'I wonder why he did that? I mean, I've seen it before.'

'If he had no business here, but just came to see you, he wouldn't bolt, would he?'

'He might have thought you were my husband.'

'Have you got one?'

'No. But I don't know what he thinks, do I?'

'Abstract. You could twist anybody's intentions, thinking like that.'

'Oh, I do, too,' she said. 'I can argue so they don't know which way they're looking.'

'I bet.'

We were standing at the spot where the leaper had gone over and out of sight. As I said, he had not jumped, but had gone down on stepping over, so that I reckoned he had thrown himself sharply down head-first, caught the edge of the cliff with the toes of his shoes and so pivoted himself underneath the projecting cliff edge, landing with his hands in one of the crevices.

Clearly, then, he had had that way of escape carefully reconnoitred, and if it was to be assumed he was previously a stranger to that area then he had been given a very exact location of that escape route.

In short, whoever had sent him had reckoned he might need a sharp, quick unfollowable way out.

So what had Percy been there for? Why should his job need the cover of instant escape?

Tregarrok was away across the field, and the combe to the house that sliced down through the cliff to the tiny beach—to the left along the shore as we stood there then, looking to the sea—was a quarter of a mile along.

It might have meant that the crack under the cliff was so deep as almost to provide a tunnel which would let Percy up and away right beyond our sight.

'Why did he bunk?' she said, repeating her earlier puzzlement. 'I mean if he came here to see me he could have made some excuse if he thought you were my husband—said he was selling brushes or something. You know. It's so easy. But to bunk like that...'

'Which identified him at once,' I said.

'Well, yes of course. I didn't realise...'

'Is it a difficult trick for someone else to do?' I said.

'Well, it's practice and nerve. If you're that way inclined—yes; you can do it. If you haven't got quite the nerve, you'll burst your noggin.'

'Did you recognise him at the window?' I said.

'Well—it was only a flash, wasn't it? But with that and his jump, yes—I'm sure.'

'It might have been another man with the same stunt?'

'Looking like Percy, you mean? Well, yes, I suppose ... You've gone and fogged me up now.' She pouted rather crossly.

'So you're not quite sure?'

She turned her nose up.

'Yes, I am sure. It was Percy.'

I looked back to the farmhouse just in behind the windbreak of trees behind the stone hedge.

'I wish I knew where he came out,' I said. 'Pity the dogs aren't here.'

'I want tea,' she said, and walked off towards the farmhouse. 'You come when you've finished sniffing.'

'I'm coming,' I said.

As I followed her to the gate I felt she was in some considerable danger, because a lot of what was planned to take place at Tregarrok was now tied up with her.

She had been at the gaming club with Percy, who had defected, cleaned out the establishment and then vanished.

Now he had turned up at the farm.

At that same club she had met Toby, who had come down to Tregarrok with her, and spotting the house had deliberately jammed the gates against further vehicles, thus showing he had known what was planned for that place.

And after he had done it, he had departed, leaving the girl to pick up the ticket for what he had done.

From that I had to assume she didn't know anything about Tregarrok and it's criminal hangers-on.

With all due respect to the charm and vivacity of the dear girl, there is nothing more dangerous and incommoding in a criminal activity than an over-confident ignoramus tripping over something at the wrong moment.

It starts shooting, in which quite often all involved get hurt, especially the innocent.

I had no way of getting her off the scene without telling her what I was there for, and, for someone with such chattiness as she to know my business might be disastrous.

At the house door she turned back suddenly.

'You don't think he might have come up near here, do you?' she said.

'I don't know. That's why I wish the dogs would appear.'

She looked down towards the field gate.

'I wonder where she got to? She's been hours.'

We went into the kitchen again.

'Did you expect her back at any particular

time? I thought you said . . .'

'I mean she ought to be back now. What's for food? I don't know what she's got in mind. If I do one thing it's bound to be the other. You know what sisters are. They only agree when they disagree. Shakespeare said that.'

'Shakespeare didn't. But he's not a bad bet, whatever you're talking about.' I looked around the big stone room. 'She left it very tidy.'

'I've never seen so much tidiness—not in this place. You'd think she was off. I mean, all this tidying looks like a last will and testament—for her, anyway.'

'She's not usually tidy?'

'Of course not. She's natural. Stuff left all over the place . . .' She turned and looked at me. 'I thought you said you knew her?'

'I do. But our association didn't include washing up.'

'Oh,' she said. 'You weren't here long, then.'

'I don't want to be alarmist, but I'm a peculiar thinker.'

'Well, that's an original start. Get on. What?'

'If she had an accident, what would the dogs do?'

'Stay with her and bark like beggary.'

'And if they were shut in the car?'

'She's got an old Land-Rover and never has the top up. The dogs wouldn't stay in it unless she said.'

'Suppose she did say?'
'Well, they'd stay, I suppose.'
She poured some more tea.
'What makes you think something might have happened? What kind of accident?'
'It was Percy who made me think of it. He looked in here for something, and finding something he didn't expect, bolted.'
'I wouldn't bother about Percy. Outside of stunts, he's a twit.'
'He did a pretty good raid on your club that night.'
'Yes. I was surprised at that, I must say. Anyway, don't worry about Freddie. She has fits of doing things. We're all a bit erratic. You might say barmy. You might have noticed it?'
'No.'
'You've worried me now,' she said, turning to the door. 'I wonder if something did happen to her? Shall we go and see?'
'I thought you said she'd gone to Mar.'
'I meant for us to look at the farm.'
'All right.'
We got back into the car and drove off, turning left outside the field gate. A short way along there was the entrance to the old farm and its ruined house in a clump of trees. We stopped on the grass by the roadside.
The cows were scattered round the fields, munching.
There was no sign of the vehicle Freddie had used to get here.

'She must have gone to Mar,' said the girl. 'Perhaps she was late leaving or something. I mean, there are no dogs here, are there?'

'They may be round the back,' I said.

'You're persistent, aren't you?' she said.

'I get ideas,' I said, and opened the gate. 'Just like to look around when somebody seems to be overdue.'

'But Freddie's always late!' she said, following me. 'We're all always late. It's a feature of the family. The only on-timer was Auntie Maud, and she was later. Uncle Joe . . . What's the matter?'

I had stopped a moment.

'You'd better stay here. Somebody's dead. It doesn't look nice.'

2

'Let me look,' she said and went past me. She stopped. 'Oh, I see what you mean.'

I went to the body, which lay in a small clearing in a clump of overgrown gorse close to the trees. The man lay face down, having been blasted in the back by a shotgun from not very far behind him.

For some reason I thought it might be Percy, who had come up from his earth at the wrong place, but it wasn't.

When I bent and had a look I recognised the man I had seen watching me in my woods at home.

There was no great mystery as to why he

should have been here, because he had worked near here. But the last time I had seen him he had been obviously spying, keeping a lookout for me forty miles away from the spot where he then lay.

'Do you know who it is?' she whispered, as if the dead man might hear her.

'I've seen him before. Working on a farm near here.'

'What was he doing at this one?'

'I don't know.'

She whispered so that I could hardly hear.

'You're not going to call the police, are you?'

There my problem had been stated for me, but to agree too readily with her might be to queer my own pitch in that place.

'Why not?' I said, surprised. 'It's usual, isn't it?'

'Because they will think that it was Freddie,' she said, urgently. 'I mean, she wouldn't—but they'll think so all the same. You know what they are when they think—I mean they suspect people like that...'

I didn't want to call the police, because to have them down here on Tregarrock's doorstep would be to freeze off the oncomers altogether, and they would come back when the watch had been given up.

The police, too, would not want to know at this point, and for the same reasons as mine. They hoped for a big haul of evil, with luck, and this corpse could spoil their chances.

From my point of view, the body should be left for another reason, and that was I knew the man had been spying on me in the wood that day, and I wanted to know why.

And what man or band of men had been behind his going there to spy.

Had he been spying on Freddie?

If he had, why here at the ruins of the old farm where she only grazed cattle? Why not at the Home Farm house where she lived?

'Did he come here to work for Freddie?' she said.

'He's not dressed for that, is he? He's wearing a suit and thin shoes.'

'Who is he? If you knew that you might know what he was doing here wouldn't you?'

I looked all around the fields. The only signs of life were the slowly moving, chomping cows and gulls wheeling out over the cliffs.

'I'll see if there's anything in his pocket,' I said, and bent down.

'Be careful!' she hissed, then changed her mind. 'No! You'd better not! Don't. In case . . .'

'In case what?'

'Well, you might leave clues and that—And a man said to me once, he said, "You want to be careful of . . ."'

'We've got to know something about him,' I interrupted. 'So shut up.'

She caught her breath.

'That's rude,' she said.

'For goodness' sake, don't be a child!' I said.

Now I knew well how to search a dead body, quickly, and without leaving a great deal of disturbance after me, but again I felt I had to fumble it a bit because she was gawping at the scene with eyes and mouth making three o's and she wasn't going to miss anything.

He carried just ordinary things; keys, knife, ballpoint, two paper pounds, almost one more in silver, some tattered little bills paid Cash, and a driving licence.

'Daniel Couch, Allway Cottage, Goose Farm, Lower Doman,' I read out. 'Any help?'

'Well, I know Lower Doman. After all I was born in that wrecked house behind you. But I never saw him before. He wasn't one of our casual workers.'

I turned to the old house. The stone walls were still sound, but the roof had collapsed in places and stood against the sky like the ribs of a skeleton.

'I'll just take a look round,' I said. 'Go and wait for me in the car.'

'Not on your life!' she said, moving away from the corpse. 'I'm sticking right by you. I've got to a point where I don't trust anything.'

'You'll be in the way,' I said.

'There's a gallant for you,' she said sarcastically. 'But I'll overlook it. Go on. Take a look round and be quick.'

She trailed close behind as I had a quick look into the house. I saw no sign that anyone had been in there for weeks. Most of the doors of the sheds and outbuildings were open, but two close to the house were shut.

When I tried them, both appeared to be locked.

'Who's got the keys to these doors?' I said. 'Do you know?'

'Well, Freddie, I would think, but I don't know. I suppose she kept the keys. She did live here a bit after Daddy died.'

'Big, old keys,' I said, looking at the keyholes. 'Big iron ones...'

'Hey, just a minute. I remember now. There used to be a big hook just inside the kitchen. I'll show you.'

We went in at the back door of the house, treading on the bits of fallen plaster and wood strewn on the stone floor.

She looked around and pointed to a big wall hook, but there was nothing on it.

'Well, they used to be there,' she said. 'Unless somebody went out to unlock something, of course.'

I went to the old dresser built against the far wall and opened one of the three drawers. There were two boxes of sporting cartridges, one full, the other with four missing.

'Does Freddie keep her cartridges here?' I said.

'I shouldn't think so. She only comes to bring the cattle. I mean, there's nothing left here but the grazing. Everything was taken over to Home Farm.'

She didn't press the subject and I shut the drawer and opened the next. An old ball of string, half unwound and tangled, some staples, an old bent spoon and a knife without a handle.

The last drawer had quite a lot of rubbish in it, apparently piled in without any reason or order. I reached under the mass of ancient papers, invoices, skewers, catalogues and old calendars and searched the bottom with my fingers.

I found a few old nails, an ancient cheap wristwatch and nothing else, but I was suspicious of the weight of the motley mass of stuff which had been piled in there and with a hand underneath and one on top I lifted the whole lot out and put it on the dresser above the drawers.

As I was about to put the heap down something slipped out of it and crashed to the ground. I dropped the heap on the dresser and picked up the heavy metal object.

'You've found the keys?' she said.

'No. I've found an automatic pistol and what's more...' I slipped out the magazine, '... it's fully loaded.'

'It can't be Freddie's!' she snapped the words out.

'Why not?' I really wanted to know if she knew it couldn't be, rather than probe into an automatic reflex on her part.

'She's got a pair of guns,' she said. 'What on

earth would she want with a thing like that? What good would it be—on a farm? Use your head!'

I put the gun on the dresser and looked in the rest of the pile of old paper rubbish. The keys were there, just three big iron ones on a ring.

'Right,' I said, and turned to her.

She stood staring at the pistol.

'What are you going to do about that gun?' she said, and pointed.

'Well, if it is Freddie's I won't touch it.'

'It can't be! I tell you! Or do you mean that man out there was shot with it?'

'No. He was killed by a shotgun.'

'Oh, lord!'

'There are lots of shotguns besides Freddie's. Besides why should she shoot anybody?'

'It's just she's a bit quick off the mark sometimes,' she said slowly. 'I mean, she'll say something like "You get out, I'll count up to three and then shoot". Well, she'll count up to three and then she feels she's in duty bound to shoot. I mean, when you say that, what else is there to do?'

'I tell you what we'll do,' I said. 'Take the ammo out.'

I unclipped the magazine again, took out the rounds, then put the empty case back and the gun back in the paper pile which I then stuffed back into the drawer.

'How do you know so much about those

guns?' she said, with a sharp look.

'It's my hobby,' I said. 'I belong to a pistol club. Target shooting.'

'Oh. Very convenient,' she said.

We went out to the outbuildings. The first one contained nothing more sinister than farm chemicals which it was wise to lock up in case children got in.

I locked the door again and opened the next.

'What's that?' she said.

'It looks like oxygen cutting equipment. Does anybody do any repairs to the tractors or the ploughs—you know, mend broken bits and pieces?'

'Oh no, they don't do that any more,' she said. 'Freddie hires them with a man and if anything goes wrong with it, he takes it back or they come out with another one.'

'Then whose is this? It's recently been used.'

'How do you know that?'

'It's gathered no moss. Look. The apparatus there is clean where it's been handled.'

She stared at me then.

'I don't know about you,' she said. 'You seem to notice such a lot. It isn't natural.'

'But that's a surveyor's job, dear,' I said, looking very patient. 'What would be the good of employing one if he didn't spot the small cracks, flaking, discolouring in the house you want to buy?'

She scratched her chin very lightly.

'I must say you're a big one with the

excuses,' she said. 'Every one a winner.'

She turned away. I took a closer look in the shed.

The cutter was a very strange find in such a place, when the main alley of suspicion was at Tregarrok. If anyone suspected the loot had been stashed in a strong room there, then the cutting equipment would have been taken there.

Tregarrok had more hiding places than half a town of normal buildings, and one could leave a dozen sets of equipment hidden around the place without much danger of anybody finding one.

But why here in a ruined farmhouse, where the farmer used only the grazing round it?

'Is there a cellar under the house?' I said.

'No,' she said, looking back. 'What would it be for?'

'Of course,' I said, and relocked the door.

'Well? Solved the mystery?'

'I wish I knew the mystery of your sister,' I said. 'You do realise that until we see her and ask if she knows anything about the man out there, we're hiding a murder. Accessories after the fact.'

'Yes. I know.' She was worried.

I began to wonder if her faith in her sister was beginning to crumble. If it did, then I had cause to worry, too.

CHAPTER FOUR

1

The girl turned to me suddenly.

'Let's go back,' she said. 'I don't want to stay here. It's beginning to make me feel sick.'

'It's a tricky situation,' I said.

'Murder is always tricky and sticky, too,' she said. 'It's bad luck standing by corpses, I'm sure. Freddie might be back, anyhow.'

There was no point in staying around a murder spot with a girl who has started to get the jumps, so I agreed. We went back to my car at the gate.

As we reached it I saw several cows ambling towards us.

'Looks as though it's coming up to milking time,' I said. 'She should be back for that.'

'Never misses,' said her sister, getting in the car. 'You can't you know.'

'And what if she does?'

'Well I know how!' she said sharply. 'I'm a farmer's daughter, too, you know!'

'I just thought you might have forgotten,' I said, and got in beside her. 'So if she doesn't turn up, something must have gone wrong.'

'She'll have to drive them back first, of course,' she said. 'That takes a while ... She *must* be home now. She wouldn't leave it too late.'

But when we got back to the Home Farm

house, it was as we had left it an hour or so before.

'Look,' she said, her mood of anxiety growing stronger, 'I'd better go and get those cows.'

'Can I help? I've done it before.'

'It's all right. I'll take the pony. He knows that lot and their funny ways.' She went out.

I looked after her to the stable, where she went in and reappeared with the saddle and bits and pieces slung on her shoulder and arm. She put two fingers in her mouth and whistled shrilly.

The pony, then at the far corner of the big field, turned from chewing grass, looked up and then galloped across to her.

She saddled up and was quickly away out of the farm gate and clopping along the road back to the murder farm. I think she felt she had to get the cows out of that place in case they somehow revealed the presence of that dead man—if presence is the word—to some passer-by looking over the hedge.

When she had gone I went back into the house. The tidiness we had earlier remarked on seemed the stranger when I was alone there. It did look as if Freddie had decided to go, cleared up everything, left it right, then gone.

But she wouldn't have left the cows.

Unless she was just prepared to land the lot in her sister's lap, but I did not think she would have trusted the wayward girl that far.

After all, the sister was now a town-girl and likely to bounce back up there at the first call from an attractive boy friend, cows or none.

I knew the house well from my previous visit and made a quick run over it. There was nothing unusual there to be seen but the extreme tidiness of the kitchen.

The cleanliness made me think that something must have happened there which had made a mess and so a rapid and thorough clean up had been necessary.

The usual reason for such an action is to try and cover the signs of a crime having been committed, though the unusual cleanliness would always make an official suspect it right from the start.

Having been alerted by the tidying, I next looked round the scullery for signs of the cleaning weapons and found them bright, shining and even cleaner than the kitchen. Even the mop head looked as if it had been carefully washed in some extra strong detergent.

I had come back into the kitchen when there was a knock out on the front door, and somebody walked in. The caller obviously heard me and came to the kitchen door.

It was Congle's agent, James Haigh. He stopped still when he saw me.

'Oh! Mr Blake,' he said. 'I expected to see you at Tregarrok.'

'I couldn't get the car in,' I said. 'The gate's

blocked. I came here to see if they knew anything about it. I know Miss Lawrence, but she isn't here.'

He looked round.

'She's usually here,' he said. 'In fact, I came for the same reason. To find out who jammed that damned boat in the gateway. It's the only vehicle entrance.'

'I saw Miss Lawrence's sister. She said somebody was trying to turn the boat round.'

'Then went off and left it?'

'She said it was brought down for her, but it's no use where it is. She seemed worried about it, but of course, she wasn't to know anybody would want to get a vehicle in there. It can't be a common occurrence from what I've seen of the place.'

'It's derelict,' he said. 'I don't think you'll ever get a grant big enough to put it right.'

'The eventual grant isn't my affair. I'm here to estimate how much it might have to be. If it's too large, perhaps the house will just be left to fall down.'

'We might get a buyer some day,' said Haigh. 'After all, there are still some rich people left in the world.'

'But few left here,' I said. 'I don't think you'd find a sheik keen on Tregarrok. After all, it's a hodgepodge, a thing of bits and pieces all shambled together over five hundred years without any plan. A potentate wanting to spend such a sum would want a palace, not a

Cornish puzzle.'

'You're not trying to sell it,' he said ironically.

'But it never has been sold, has it? Handed down and down, generation to generation, ending up with an old woman who lives alone in Scotland and has even forgotten it still exists.'

'You know all that?'

'I know Mr Congle.'

'Of course. Yes. That crooked business. Pretty horrible. It didn't connect. Of course, it was you who was here when they found all those dead bodies. I've always wondered if there was any sane criminal reason for that slaughter.'

'Well, they weren't killed to please the Sunday papers.'

'Did you see any of it?'

'It happened while I was here—the finding of the death pit. When I thought I had been in there, thinking of starting to measure up when that lunatic was prowling around—perhaps he had even been behind me—I felt a bit weak at the knees. I don't mind thunder, but I do mind blood.'

'Oh, you hadn't started work there?'

'No. I hadn't even found my way round in there—if there is a way round. I did think of tying a string to the main staircase and then exploring. That would have made sure I got back to the front door.'

He did not seem to be listening. His mind was on something else.

I was trying to play the innocent, but I knew quite well he had come because Congle had sent him. Congle would have wanted to make sure what I was doing there.

On my previous visit I had found the death pit, but had kept the evidence so that the finding had been an accident—which in fact, it was—although I had been looking for something of the sort. At no time in the evidence had I said I had been doing anything but preparing a survey, because there had been the suspicion at the time that the matter was not cleared up.

At the trial, however, it seemed that it was, but then, the prosecution weakness lay in the fact that the chief villain had killed himself and therefore a great deal of evidence which certainly would have been got from him was lost with him.

But Congle had been well in it and the fact that he had been set free was lack of evidence, and that lack could have been made up if the chief villain had been alive.

Now Congle was back, and immediately on his return he had seen me return, too. I did not think there was much doubt as to what he would think about that coincidence, but my difficulty then was to place Haigh.

If he was straight, then Congle would have told him nothing except to keep an eye on me for the good of the estate.

But if he wasn't, Congle would have told him a great deal.

'The girl lives here all alone, doesn't she?' he said, looking round the kitchen.

'She farms it. As I said, the sister's staying, but she lives in London, I gather. She came down to receive the boat.'

'Well, she's received that all right. What I want to know is what she's going to do about it?'

'From what I could see it'll be an expert job without wrecking the boat and the gate.'

'Bad as that, is it?' He looked startled. 'I'd better have another look. I didn't realise . . .' He went towards the door. 'Will you tell Miss Lawrence I will come back?'

'Certainly.'

He went. I didn't hear a car start for quite a time, so he must have left it some way off which explained why I had not heard it arrive.

Again I looked round the tricky clean kitchen. If anything had been left behind I knew it would have to be very small.

When suspicious of cleanliness one's natural suspicion is murder, but murder is a large affair and clearing up after it takes a long time. In the first place, to clear the decks one must remove the corpse, and that implies having a prepared place ready to receive it which isn't going to be seen from anyone passing outside.

Second, there is the mess of murder. If it is by

shooting, knifing or bludgeoning there is bound to be blood, which is a Big Mess and very difficult to clean up. If it is something physical, like strangulation, there is going to be the mess of struggle somewhere, upon something.

Which leaves poison. If this is used it is usual for the receptacle, teacup, wineglass, or what else to be washed up together with two or three more and stood on the draining board. It is usual to find some washed up things on draining boards, or dirty things in sinks. They would attract no attention.

But to clean the whole kitchen afterwards, including the tools you cleaned it with, is to draw attention.

And that is just what it had done.

Freddie had taken the cows to the old farm and from there had intended to go into Mar on some business or the other. If that had been known to the cleaner, he would probably have known roughly how long her business would take her, and so be sure of time enough to do his work in the kitchen and to clean up carefully after.

Excellent, as far as that. But what about the jolly sister?

If there had been so clean a planner as I had in mind for this short time, surely he must have thought of her?

Unless she had been in with the cleaner.

In *what*?

She had been with Percy the great stunt man who went in for sudden, unexpected crimes like clearing all the money off the gambling tables while the audience was looking for his mangled body somewhere down in the street. He had done the same trick—without money—on the cliff edge.

But if he had done such a wonderful cleaning job, why risk being found out by coming back to peer through the window?

Unless he had been in it with Laura, his occasional stunt partner.

Now she had gone off to fetch the cows leaving me to poke around in there and find out what they had been up to. That didn't seem like guilt.

Furthermore I was here because it was believed that considerable dough or its equivalent was still lying about attracting vultures.

But if there was any such it would be at Tregarrok, not at a small farmhouse where the occupier might find some trace of it any day.

Then it occurred to me that there was a reason for washing everything as a cover up. That was that some part of the room had been cleaned, and by itself it showed up too much like the proverbial sore thumb.

Which meant that in the first place the cleaned part of the room might have been part of a big part; a big unbroken part where it would be noticeable.

But the big, slate flagged floor was the only unbroken part that would fill that bill.

I looked down. The flags were big, though of varying sizes, and even the big ones were not large enough to form a temporary grave cover.

A slow walk over the floor did not show any disturbed joints between the stones, no new cement. I turned and looked at the stove set in the great wide mouth of the chimney breast.

And then I realised what must have been the reason, just as I heard cows lowing almost outside the open house door and then Laura's voice calling to me urgently.

2

I went out. The cows were ambling into their shed on the left. Laura was on the pony and pointing across to the great dark house.

'Look! The dogs!'

The two setters, red and white, could be seen running like mad on the grass past the end of the big house, heading for the stone wall hedge between the grounds and the farm. They went out of sight below the hedge, then appeared suddenly on the top of it and leapt down on our side. They ran on towards us wagging their tails as they came nearer, but passed us, went to the house door and then lay down, panting, their heads turned to look the way they had come.

'You know what?' the girl said. 'She's sent them back!'

'From where?'
'You saw.'
'I only saw them pass the end of the house. You saw them before that.'
'The other side of the Combe,' she said. 'In the trees there. I wonder why she did that?'
'In trouble?'
'I don't know. She does do it sometimes. It's good training. But if she was threatened, I don't think they'd leave her.'
'I'll get over there,' I said. 'I've got to get in there sooner or later.'
The cows were mooing restlessly from inside the shed and round the front of it.
'I'd better start on this lot,' she said, turning the pony. 'Give me a whistle if you find her.'
'I couldn't get the dogs to come?'
'Not once she's sent them back. They'll wait till kingdom come till she says go.'
I went off across the field towards the wall. The grounds on the other side looked deserted. The trees around the top of the combe were thickening with green, and they had grown so close together that I could see nothing beyond or even in amongst them.
Ahead of me the path from the house ran across, began to go down into the combe and vanished behind the trees. As I went towards it, someone came towards me.
She came with long purposeful strides, her wide slacks flapping. Her shirt pushed out militantly, and her head, close cropped in man

fashion, looked a little too small by comparison with the rest.

She did not seem surprised to see me but came right up and offered a hand to shake.

'Poxon,' she said. 'Boat builder.'

'Blake,' I said. 'Surveyor.'

'Oh, I thought you must be Mr Haigh,' she said. 'He rang me. I came at once.'

'He was here. Looking at the boat,' I said, and wondered why, if she had come to examine the boat, she was so far away from it.

Unless she had come up from the beach. But the path along the combe to the little rocky cove below had had a bridge half way, and that had collapsed a long time ago. I could not imagine it having been repaired, or any reason for a repair since officially, nobody lived at Tregarrok and there was no prospect of anyone moving in.

'You've just arrived then?'

'By a devious route—yes. The difficulty, I believe, is that the boat is valuable and so is the gate. The gate is rather special?'

'It would be difficult to get another made like it. You see that the spikes on the top of the uprights depict various stages in the history of the estate. In my opinion the gates should have been taken down and stored and some other gates put up there, but there it is.'

'Nothing has been looked after, has it?' She looked at the house.

'No. That's why I'm here. To see what needs

to be done.'

'I got in over a wall way back there,' she said and turned to point directly behind her. 'Couldn't even get in the gate on foot. It's a mess.'

'I came over the opposite wall. I knew the farmer here. I thought she was here, as a matter of fact. Chasing some stray animals.'

She looked round again. 'I didn't meet anyone. But it's a big place. She, you said?'

'Yes, Miss Lawrence. She farms that land.'

'I think the only way to shift that boat,' she said, putting her hands on her hips, 'is to hire a crane and lift the stern up vertically. Something will tear, but it will be local damage. Once we've got it in the air we can back the crane across the road and the trailer will follow till the boat is quite clear of the gate.'

'It will have to be a biggish crane.'

'Yes. That's no difficulty, the only thing is you have to book them ahead so we wouldn't get it for a day or two. Does that matter to you?' She cocked her head.

She was a very handsome lady, about thirty-five, very fair, green eyes and peach complexion with just a little tan. What attracted me was the side look at me which revealed a sparkling amused light in the eyes and a slight hitch at the corners of her full lips.

'It won't affect me. I'm parked over at the farm. I can hitch my stuff across.'

'Strange that a place so big should have only

one proper entrance.'

'It was deliberate and carefully maintained that way,' I said. 'It meant that if there was pursuit by the coastguard, excise men, the army or other public body their entry was restricted.'

She began to laugh. 'Oh, is that it? I see now you point it out, the drystone walls round the grounds here are quite broken. I suppose once they were too high for a horse to jump?'

'I should think so.'

At first I had had the thought she had met me with the idea of restricting my pursuit, so that by the time I went on looking for Freddie she wouldn't be there.

But the woman's attitude and the dogs made me think otherwise. The dogs had been sent back by Freddie; nobody else could have done it, and therefore she had wished them to go, and that must have meant she wanted to do something where the dogs would not be seen and give her away.

In other words, if there was danger, she was making it herself, of her own choice, and it might be that she would not welcome a noisy knight to the rescue.

'You're in the boat business?' I said.

'Boat building and repairs at Mar. My ex-husband is head of the firm but he's always going on round the world sea trips to advertise the boats. He is away so often I get lonely, but if married, I must be faithful, so we unmarried and I can do what I like without contravening the concubines' charter.'

It was all said in such a matter of fact manner I laughed, and so did she.

'Do you know this place?' I said.

She looked at the house again and shook her head.

'Pretty glum pile,' she said. 'No. I know of it, but what's here for anyone to come by for?'

So she didn't know it, but Haigh had left me only a short time ago, and in that period he had got to a phone, rung her, and she had got in a vehicle, come up here, seen the boat, gone round to find a reasonable way in over a broken wall, and then met me.

'When did Haigh ring you?' I said.

'Oh, a couple of hours back. I don't rush unless a boat's sinking, and this one can't.' She chuckled.

Which meant that Haigh had known all about the true boat situation before he had met me at the farm. It didn't really matter, because I had suspected him, anyhow, of being a Congle man and a Congle man was anything that wasn't straight.

On the other hand, I realised that it was only her attractiveness that had softened my suspicion of her.

Then I realised I had come because of Freddie, and at the time of arrival had found Laura not without allure, and then I thought that Spring was softening up my judgement of feminine suspects.

'Take me to look inside,' she said suddenly, looking at the black house. 'I feel it must be like a Black Museum.'

'You read about it when they found the bodies?'

'Oh yes. But they took them all away, didn't they?'

'Yes. The keys are over in my car. I'll fetch them.'

'Do,' she said, and smiled.

I turned and went back to the farmhouse where my car was standing outside. I got the keys and as I shut the door a voice called from the house door.

'Hey. She's back,' Laura said.

The dogs were still there and I said so.

'She told them to stay,' said the girl.

'Okay. I'll just pop in and see her. I've got to go back to the house.'

I walked along by the side of the house to the milking shed. A few cows were wandering away, looking for a quiet munch. The milking machine motor was humming away very quietly. I went into the long shed. The lights were on, six cows were connected up but no one was there.

I called out, and there was no answer. I looked round and Laura came up behind me.

'What's the matter?' she said.

'She isn't here.'

'Oh crumbs. She's got wanderlust today. I

don't know what's the matter with her. I'd better see to the rest. You go over to the house. She'll be back when you do and I'll sit on her to stop her drifting.'

I went back over the broken wall towards the house. The woman was not in sight, but I thought she would most likely be waiting near the main door which, even for all the odd bits and pieces that comprised the building, was unmistakeable.

When I got round there, no one was about.

I looked all round, from the trees near the gate to the wood in which the combe cut down, and saw no one at all.

It was beginning to look like a day of the Disappearing Women. I could think of no reason why they should do so, but I knew it was a very bad place in which to do it.

A number of people had disappeared in this place not so long ago, and they had been found only by accident.

I tried the main door, the heavy keys in my left hand, just in case the door was, after all, unlocked. It was.

I went into the great hall. It was so still it seemed as if the dust was holding it down.

And then I heard the sound of a shot which I recognised. It was a revolver shot and it had come from one of the corridors leading off the hall.

CHAPTER FIVE

1

The sound of the shot was not far off, for the echoes which followed it along those tortuous corridors were faint by comparison.

As I crossed the hall I heard somebody running. I looked towards the corridor entrance near the foot of the stairs just as Poxon came running out, wearing only trousers. She ran to me, flung her arms round my waist and looked back towards the corridor, twisting her frightened head as far as it could go.

'He tried to shoot—that man—' she gasped for breath, but I thought she was short of it from fright more than exercise.

'Easy,' I said, patting her bare back. 'What man?'

'I don't know.' She shuddered. 'He came up behind me. I didn't hear anything at all. Suddenly he grabbed my shoulder. I heard him start to say something, and then I just ran. He had his grip so hard he tore my shirt off. It just burst. I ran quite a way then he fired after me . . . fired a gun!'

She became still, tensed up, then let go a big breath and relaxed a little.

'Sorry to throw a forty-inch bust at you, but I wasn't going back for my shirt,' she said, and managed a smile as she let me go.

'Have my jacket,' I said. I slipped it off and gave it to her though she looked much better as she was. I kept a sly watch on the corridor but there was no movement in its dark maw.

Her shout when she had seen me must have been heard by him, so that he knew someone was with her. In such circumstances a gunman in the shadows would back off and survey the situation again.

Trying to chase him in that labyrinthine house would be a waste of time. One might run across him anywhere, and he could be just as easily behind as in front of you.

In collecting my gear from the car I had included my pistol, but there is no profit in starting a shooting match until you can see the enemy, and even then it doesn't always pay.

I had hoped that out of curiosity to see whom she was with he might have shown himself, just for a quick look, but as he did not, I had to assume he knew.

He must have been very intent on keeping her, for to burst a shirt off the wearer takes some doing, though in a violent short struggle she might instinctively have wriggled the shirt off to get away. Either way, his grip must have been formidable.

The shot then, had been a scarer, so he had believed at the time she had been alone or he wouldn't have fired it.

'Do you remember what he started to say?' I went a step nearer the corridor entrance.

'Something about "Don't try..." I think it was.'

'And you didn't see anything?'

'It's very gloomy in there. In fact I'd wandered in there to see what the place was like, but just decided to turn back, because of the dark. It's eerie down there. Smells of death—dust—You know—Mummies' wrappings. I've got the horror film complex in this place. Sorry.'

'You'd just turned back when he grabbed you?'

'Yes. Yes—I think I had, just that moment.'

'So he must have been in front of you before that.'

'No, I think he must have been at the side. Those panels and armour and stuff, all half collapsed. Anyone could be hiding there, yet, because I began to feel fluttered, I kept near the side instead of staying in the middle.'

'It's possible he thought you'd seen him and turned to go back,' I said.

'*I* scared *him*?' she said, surprised. 'Well, I certainly didn't think of it that way round!' Then she laughed, but stopped again. 'Well, we'd better tell the police.'

'I don't think they'd believe it,' I said. 'There are all sorts of stories about this place, all unsavoury, some ghostly, some bloody as hell, and anyone knowing such things might be very nervous and imaginative coming in here, specially when exploring a dark corridor without a light.'

'You think they'd think I was drunk?'

'No, just plain imagining things. When I started work here some months ago a visitor came and got shot by his own imagination. It's a pity your story is much the same. And the reputation of the building is much worse now. You probably went to look and see if you could find where the death pit was.'

She chuckled.

'Well, how did you guess?'

'There you are. You strung yourself to too high a pitch to start with.'

'Where's my shirt?'

'I think it's down the corridor. The man would be mad to take it.'

'Well, let's see.'

So we went down the gloomy corridor. The small-paned windows along one side were so thick with dust and webs that any light was filtered about six times on the way through.

There were some old things as she'd said, suits of armour which had collapsed into huddled dwarfs, along the other side. When we stopped still there was dead quiet in the whole place. It seemed to be totally insulated from the outside world.

The shirt lay on the floor in the middle of the corridor, quite a way ahead.

'You go ahead and fetch it,' I said quietly.

She looked askance at me, then nodded and went ahead with long strides, as if quite confident. I watched very carefully as she bent and picked up the shirt, then turned and came back, examining the shirt for damage as she came.

I saw nothing of anyone there, but just ahead of where the shirt had lain there was a junction to a passage on the right.

'All the buttons off,' she said. 'And that's all.'

'As we were saying just now, it's not hard to bust the shirt open and the buttons off with one's own hands, for purposes of exhibitionism.'

'You needn't worry,' she said with an odd look, 'but I don't want to go to the police. It does go on so. Once you've got a complaint on their books it gets more of a nuisance to you than whatever happened in the first place.'

'I was thinking more along the lines of some drunken layabout getting in here with a shotgun. The door was unlocked.'

'Don't worry,' she said, a little shortly. 'I won't call the police.'

'I'm not worrying,' I said. 'But if they come they'll have to seal it off and look for the shot somewhere down there and I'll have my work put off for days, and I don't see I can fit it in again for weeks.'

'Oh, I see,' she said, with a smile. 'I was beginning to think you were some robber baron on the run.'

'Not rich enough,' I said. 'Regretfully.'

'Oh, you're rich enough,' she said, with sudden come-togetherness and put her arm through mine as we walked together out of the corridor with the shirt dangling against her knees.

I had been apprehensive about illicit wanderers in the rambling house, and worried about what had happened to Freddie. I should have connected both together, and worried and been apprehensive.

For as we walked together into the great hall, me in shirt-sleeves and she in my jacket, bare beneath and her shirt hanging like a past joy from her jolly hand, Freddie suddenly walked in at the front door.

'Oh!' she said, seeing us. 'All right, then?' She turned and would have walked out but she walked straight into her sister Laura, who was behind her.

'Oh,' said Laura, just in view. 'It's a grapple.'

'Oh, don't be so primitive!' cried Poxon, furiously. 'What children are these. Yours?' She turned and glared at me.

'These are my friends,' I said, and introduced them, but no one took much notice except to sniff and look aloof, and that did put the idea in my mind that, though they might not know one another, they had seen if not met.

'Laura is the owner of the boat,' I said.

'Oh yes,' said Poxon. She took off my jacket and put on the shirt. 'I've come to see about getting it off the spikes. Have you got a safety pin?'

'Try a spike,' said Freddie, and looked at me. 'I heard you wanted to see me. I suppose it doesn't matter now.'

'Business always matters,' I said. 'But the papers are over in my car.' There were no papers in my car to do with her, but even non-existent they would hold the interest.

'Oh, I didn't know it was business,' said Laura.

'Don't mention it,' said Poxon, and I knew she meant the assault.

'Don't thank me,' said Laura, staring.

'I had a bag,' said Poxon, looking round. 'I must have dropped it up there.' She marched back into the corridor.

'Funny, forgetting a bag,' said Freddie, looking at me.

'This has been a stressful occasion,' I said. 'Have you seen anybody around this house in the last few days?'

'No. But not long ago I did.'

'And you sent the dogs back?'

'Yes. They get a little too inquisitive sometimes.'

'There's been a shooting here. Nobody hurt. No fuss necessary. That's why I'd like to know who you saw.'

'The woman you were playing about with.'

Laura was smiling quietly as she looked around the great hall.

'What was she doing?' I said.
'She was using a posh camera.'
'Taking pictures of what?'
'She was photographing the bank a little way down the combe. From what I could see there were only some bushes and trees there, but she kept clicking like a machine gun.'
The woman came back, her shirt pinned and the big bag in her hand. It was a leather satchel bag, and she had not had it when I had met her outside as she had walked up to me from amongst the trees fringing the combe.
The camera she had used was probably in it, so I assumed she had had it with her in the combe, so when she had met me, she must have left the bag in the bushes there.
I was prepared to suspect anybody during my visit to Tregarrok, but she had told a story of being a local boatbuilder which was too easily checked to be a lie. Almost any local person would know whether she was or not.
The villains expected were not local; far from it. And Laura's boy friend had known who they were, and he came from London.
'It fell behind one of those chests along the passage there,' said Poxon, and put the bag on the long refectory table. 'I suppose it came off with my shirt.'
'Just fancy not noticing,' said Laura with quiet amusement.
'Shall we see about your boat?' said Poxon,

quietly acid. 'It's not your boat, is it?' She looked at Freddie.

'The only sort of boat I want is an ark,' said Freddie.

I put my hand on the leather bag as Poxon was turned away. Whatever was inside was either soft or flat. There was no 'posh' camera such as Freddie would have spotted from some distance away.

'Let's go and discuss it,' said Poxon, taking up her bag. She went towards the door, then stopped and looked back at Laura. 'It *is* your boat?'

'It is my boat,' said Laura. 'You go first.'

They went out. Freddie looked at me.

'Why have you come back?' she said.

'I've been chartered by a Government department this time,' I said, and explained the new surveying instructions.

She sat on the edge of the table and looked at me.

'Oh yes?' she said. 'Just that?'

'Well, of course just that,' I said. 'What else?'

'You made a bit of a diversion last time.'

'As far as I'm concerned, you did that.'

She tilted her head up.

'Oh indeed! And does the thought of me make you tear off women's shirts?'

'I did not do that,' I said. 'It was an unfortunate experience she had before I saw her.'

'You met her outside. Come off it!'

'I met her outside. She wanted to look inside. I went back to my car to get the keys. Right!'

'You say so.'

'Right. I go to my car. Your sister said you were home so I looked round for you and you weren't there. Where had you gone?'

'There was a man out on the cliff path. I wondered what he was doing.'

'Why?'

'He was staring at the farmhouse in a funny way. When I went up to the hedge, he turned and walked away.'

'You didn't know him?'

'No.'

'A man has been murdered on your old farm. Just by the house.'

She looked at me steadily.

'Laura told me. She said it made her sick.'

'It's never a good sight.'

'Who was it? Do you know? She didn't tell me. Said it made her sick again. In fact, that's why we came over here to find you. I'd have broached it before, but you were so busy stripping that fat cow . . .'

'Leave that out. It's a waste.'

'Well, who was the dead man?'

'He used to work for Congle, on the farm,' I said. 'A few days ago, he was in my grounds spying on me. Now he's dead.'

'Shot, Laura said.'

'Yes. Pretty close to, so I think it was no accident.'

She stared down at the floor.

'There have been one or two people about in the last two or three days,' she said. 'But people I've never seen before. They don't belong here.'

She slid off the table.

'I'm glad you came,' she said, and turned away. 'Purely as a bodyguard, of course.'

2

'Just what other people have you seen round here? All strangers?'

'I mean strangers. Congle's out, I know, but he hasn't shown up here. That's not surprising. He's probably shy. But I didn't see anyone who worked for him, either.'

'A friend of your sister's turned up unexpectedly when I called at your house,' I said. 'By the name of Percy.'

'I don't know a Percy, but she has so many hangers-on in town.'

I explained what this one had done, by way of profitably entertaining guests at the gaming house.

'Oh him! Yes!' Freddie said. 'She told me about him. Mad.'

I then told her what he had done on the cliff edge.

'Do you know if there's a cave that runs in under there somewhere?'

'It's probably honeycombed with them. Tregarrok has been used by seafaring villains for five hundred years. That's bound to leave a few holes.'

'It must have an outlet somewhere back from the clifftop. I wondered if you'd ever seen an opening thereabouts?'

* * *

'No. I'd have blocked it in. The cattle might fall in a hole like that, break a leg or worse. No, I'd think it more likely to come out in a hedge—you know, the drystone hedges round here? Pretty wide. Gorse on top here and there and backing up against the sides in places.'

She looked at me very sharply.

'You mean in the farmhouse, don't you? You mean the cave comes up in there?'

'That or one of the buildings. Somebody cleaned up your kitchen with very special care today.'

'My kitchen? What for?'

'To remove signs of something, I imagine.'

'Signs of what? You don't mean something horrible? There is one murder . . .'

'The place is cleaned right through, the cleaning things cleaned as well, so that there is no trace of what was cleaned up. A very thorough job.'

'Blood, do you mean?'

'That's what one thinks of at once. But no. I don't think it was blood or anything like it. Something much more sure to get in the cracks.'

'What?'

'Soot. You must have had a very special sweep there today.'

'I haven't had the sweep!'

'You have, whether you wanted it or not. Somebody has been at the chimney.'

'They must have got burnt as well as dirty. The stove's on.'

'The cooker was shut right down, and there are such things as asbestos gloves.'

'All right, all right! What on earth for? Is there something hidden up there?'

'It might be that. It might be there is an opening at the back of the cooker.'

'Okay. So anybody coming out of it gets a roast bottom. Don't be daft. You can't climb about over a hot stove.'

'Besides the gloves you might buy a sheet of asbestos of suitable size.'

'Are you a burglar after all?'

'I came for no other purpose but to tear Mrs Poxon's shirt off.'

'Oh . . . ! I forgive. All right.'

'By what right do you choose to forgive me?'

She pouted. 'Oh, I see. You want to stir it up.'

I did at the time want to carry on a conversation which had nothing to do with Tregarrok because I could see a shadow on the wall through the bannisters of the landing which ran round two sides of the great hall.

It is a principle of double crossing that if you

believe somebody nasty to be in the house, take no notice and wait till he gets impatient, and then he will move, and when anything moves it is possible to see it.

Since the shot, which might well have been an excited accident, the attacker had laid very low. That might mean one of two things; either he didn't know the way out other than by the front door, and had no wish to get lost in the maze of corridors, or he had the job of seeing what we were doing.

It seemed then it might be that the second might be the answer to the quiet period.

I kept the conversation short, sharp and quarrelsome, a combination of qualities she did not find difficult. Meanwhile an occasional glance showed the shadow slowly moving towards the stair head.

Such was the angle from my view up over the edge of the balcony that I saw nothing of the man at all. It was the low height at which the big windows were set that threw his shadow up higher than he.

Then suddenly the main doors almost burst open and Poxon marched in.

'Well, if you can't afford to get it off the spikes, how come you can afford to own a barge that size?' she demanded, then stopped, looking up.

'It was a gift,' said Laura appearing behind her.

'There's somebody up there!' said Poxon in a

clarion call. 'It must be That Man!'

From that instant the shadow disappeared. I went to the stairs and very carefully up them until I could see back down along the gallery.

There was no sign of any man then, of course, he had been given plenty of warning by the Stentorian Poxon.

As I went along I could see the three attentive faces of the women staring up. I suddenly had a comic vision of rapt children at a pantomime suddenly shouting out, 'Look out! He's behind you!'

I stopped at the first corridor leading off into the depths of the rambling house and looked along it. As on the floor below, the passage was lined with old chests, battered armour and prints that couldn't be admired for dust on the glass.

There was a movement half way along the passage, but it was mostly hidden by a lurching suit of armour and I saw but the edge of something as it shifted position.

'There's no one up here!' I called down. 'You must have imagined it, but I'll just make sure.'

I started to walk down the corridor. The edge of soft material protruding beyond the steel breastplate moved slightly. Behind where that movement happened the entrance to another passage showed about six feet away.

If the man there was going to back down to it and get away, he would need to be very sharp or very clever, because as he moved away from the armour so he would tend to show up in my line of sight.

And suddenly he did.

He walked out from behind the armour, as if on a lopsided afternoon stroll, a home made, distorted looking cigarette dangling from his fat mouth and tobacco dangling from the cigarette end. He appeared to be making notes in a very small notebook.

He pretended not to see me and turned his back.

Naturally, I wondered what the trick was then, for certainly he, fat, ungainly, unhealthy—even after a few weeks safe holding in prison—could never have held Poxon so hard he had torn her shirt off her back.

I went up to him.

'Mr Congle,' I said.

He turned in exaggerated surprise, little eyes almost popping from their fat, pouchy bags. He breathed like someone blowing through a nutmeg grater.

'Miss' Blake, is it? Yes. Yars. Yerz. Ah. Blake, yerz. I heard you hermph comin' and that. Well, be a good thing hermph get somebody to take this bloody plaze over, I'm sure. Git zick erve whole bloody thing, yerz. All faw down time ter come hurmph whatever you dooze, I zay.'

'I met Mr Haigh,' I said.

'Mr Haigh? Oh yerz,' he said and coughed

thickly. 'Daft as a brush, but rigid, oh yerz, rigid. Need rigids these days. People think its a sign er senze. Ersh.'

'You have somebody with you?' I said.

Congle looked up sharply.

'Me? Eh? No. Just freshin the memory. Bin away a bit y'know. Loss contact here and there. Yerz.'

I knew that Congle, whatever the effects of his holiday with prison care and attention, couldn't have the physical requirement of the man who had been prowling around.

'You must have left the main door open,' I said.

'Yerz, yerz. I was going out again, yerzee. Don' wanner be locked in. Never trust the locks in this place, no. Never truss anything in the bloody place, ask me, no.'

'Somebody followed you in. Probably followed you all over the place.'

His little eyes looked like marbles in mock surprise.

'No! No, no, not on. Not on a-bloody-tall. I'd ha' known. Got a noze for it. Noze. That's the thing—noze.'

'He followed you in and fired a shot downstairs. A gunshot, Mr Congle. Didn't you hear it?'

'Me? Zhot? No, no. Don'ear too well, y'know. Get gatarrh. Wax in me ears. Deafenin y'know. Don' wanner hear zhots, anyway. Bad fer the ealth. Always keep away from zhots,' he said, and began to walk away from me.

CHAPTER SIX

1

'Mr Congle!' I called. 'Just a moment.'

He turned his flabby bulk to look back at me.

'Yersh?'

'I said somebody fired a shot in here.'

'Well it dint hit me so I don wannaknow, thankz.'

'You've no idea who could have followed you?'

'Probly just found the door open. Came in. Zhot a bat. Lotser bats.' He thought a moment, then came heavily back to me. 'I tell yer, Mr Blake, I got wind about this blace since I came back. Bad wind. Get rid er this commission if I was you. I've been tryin' to get rid of it for years and it's got now so you can't tell who'll be here nex'. You know what you found when you was here before, well, I wouldn't be surprised if that wasn't a small business compared.'

'You expect something bad?'

'Bloody bad, but I do'know what. Thasser trouble. I came along to see if anything started, but there's nothin'.'

'You won't tell the police?' I almost laughed

but kept very straight.

'Me and the bolice...' he looked at the ceiling for a word, '—is orff beat. As you brobly know, they tried to accuse me and it dint come orff, which is gradifyin', but they do'n like it when they do'n win, you see the meanin'?'

'Where did you hear about this bloody bad thing that's due to happen here?'

'Well—' he considered a moment, 'I don't mind tellin' you, but there was a mizunderstandin' 'tween me and the police and I was put into gaol, if you underztand me, and all zorts of weird rumours go on in there.'

'And what was the rumour which has worried you?'

'Some people in the smoke don't think the bolice found it all. There may be a big raid, and as I'm resbonsible, sometimes I wish they hadn't let me out.'

'Your feeling's as bad as that?'

'One thing about clink,' said Congle, philosophically, 'is they look after you and nobody can get in you don't want ter see.'

'Did anyone try to get in touch with you? About the plans of the house perhaps?'

'You know there aren't any. Not a biddle in the ocean of a sniff of a drawing in existence.'

'But a stranger wouldn't know that.'

'Well you'd think a professional would find out about what he was thinkin' of blowin'. Casin' the joint—as they say in those brofessions—is the first step and it's only a fool jumps in without doin' it, and if there aint no blans of a place like this how can you do it?'

'Well, in this case they don't have to watch for the habits and times of people coming and going, as in an ordinary house, because this one's empty. They could come and take their time looking round.'

'Bud you know the blace . . .' he stopped and blew his nose, '—it's like a maze. You can go round and round the same way for a week and never find the way.'

'The only other way, Mr Congle, is the way they used before; to find someone who does know the way about this house.'

He picked his nose thoughtfully.

'Yah yah, I had that on my mind, I tell you. I did. You understand these beeble don't know that I don't know, perhaps, but to them I'd gwalify. You see that, Mr Blake? Though I don't know, I'd gwalify, and that's what I don't want to do. So I'm just refreshin' my memory of the place, and then I'm off. Fact, I'm off now.' He started to roll away like a sailor of a moving deck, then stopped and looked back. 'Take care you don' gwalify,' he added, and went on to get out of the house the back way.

I went up to the passage he had gone into and looked along it. I saw no Congle, but there was another, thinner, faster moving figure right at the end.

I saw him just silhouetted against a lattice

window before he turned to the right and vanished. I went along after him, but not to follow or catch. I wanted to see that part of the house I knew from my last visit and see if I could spot any obvious changes.

At the end of that passage I went down the stairs to a corridor below which ran along the backs of the kitchens and store rooms; fine cold places which once had stored rather more than food.

The floor was still scattered and smeared with broken lumps of old plaster which had fallen from the ceiling. They had been trodden in, but no one could tell when.

The outside door of the main kitchen was still missing and the evening light was shadowing over the trees at the boundary with the farm.

I made my way back through the corkscrew passages to the great hall. Poxon and Laura were arguing. It was a question of money.

'We must discuss it more,' said Poxon, looking round. 'It's getting too dark in here. Are there any lights?'

'No,' I said.

'Come back to the farmhouse,' said Freddie. 'You'll have to get it sorted out.'

It certainly would have to be sorted out, I understood as we walked back, for the boat was stuck on the gate, damaged. Laura, the owner, hadn't got any money, and she did not know if it was insured.

We got back into the farmhouse kitchen. Freddie poured beer all round and the discussion continued.

'Regardez vous,' said Poxon, and it sounded as if it was not the first time she asked it, 'the boat is stuck on the gate, and it is expensively damaged. Right?'

'Well, I know that, but I haven't any brass, no bread, no dough, no wad.'

'But you've got the bloody boat!' said Poxon fiercely.

'But I can't sell it stuck up on a gate!' said Laura. 'And I'm not sure I want to sell it, anyway. It's status, a boat like that.'

'Call girl status,' said Poxon, shortly.

'Take care,' said Freddie.

'Let us get down to this,' said Poxon. 'The first thing is the boat has to be got off, and for that we must hire a crane, and I doubt whether we could hire a big one for a half day, so it would be full rate for a day. That is driver and two men, plus the machine. All three men have to know what they're doing, so top rate for them, company charge five pounds an hour, eight hours, distance . . . I reckon it will cost a couple of hundred to get it off and down to my yard. Right?'

'If you mean is it all right, no. I don't have two hundred.'

'Two hundred,' said Poxon as if she had not heard. 'Right, now we've got it at the yard, and the repairs—by the look of the damage—might make it up to a thousand. Right?'

'Don't keep saying Right.' Laura sighed.

'Have you got any hire purchase on the boat?'

Laura stared blankly. 'I don't know,' she said.

'For heaven's sake! How did you buy it, or did you get it from pleasing a Rajah?'

'I won it.'

Freddie started to laugh at the sight of Poxon's face.

'What? In a competition?' said Poxon.

Laura explained. Poxon sat back.

'Are you sure it's legally yours?' she said.

'Well, I won it.'

Poxon looked at Freddie, then at me.

'I think we'd better get in touch with the loser,' she said at last.

'Well, he won't want to know,' said Laura petulantly. 'He lost it. He isn't going to pay anything now, is he?'

'He might not think he lost it,' said Poxon and added very quickly, 'that is, if he tries to wriggle out of it now. Men do change their minds after a wild night.'

'But he brought it down,' said Freddie. 'That doesn't sound like a change of mind.'

'No,' said Poxon, 'but you see my point, I don't want to be lumbered with a bad debt for a thousand quid and then hold the boat and get a writ from the owner and have to let it go and then sue you to sue him and get the money back. Oh no, the boat stays where it is, high and dry till you find out your nose from your elbow.

'I want to know, first, if it's insured; in which case the company have to come and estimate damage before they'll do anything: second, if there's any hire purchase debt on it, in which case the ship isn't yours, nor your boyfriend's, either.'

'Complications, complications,' Laura said crossly.

'Easy come, easy go,' said Freddie.

'Go!' said Laura. 'It hasn't even come yet. Stuck up there on a gate. It's the same with anything I get for nothing. Somebody always wants paying for it after.'

Her soliloquy of misery was interrupted by the dogs barking out in the hall. Freddie looked towards the door, then at me.

'I'll go,' I said. 'It's dark out there.'

It was all I could think of to say, but at least it would make Poxon and Laura wonder what I was talking about and when the brain is curious it's not so easy for a visitor to surprise it.

Freddie understood rather more of what I meant.

I looked at the window as I went to the door into the hall. It was almost dark outside.

In the hall the English Setter was sniffing eagerly at the front door, but the Irish was barking at the window set in the wall six feet away from the door.

From that it looked as if there might be more than one person out there, and one who did not intend to be seen by whoever opened the door to the caller. It is an old game for violent entry; one to stand in front and keep the attention and the other to sneak up from the side and sandbag the attention.

'Call the dogs!' I shouted so the caller could hear.

Freddie whistled sharply. Both dogs, disappointed and perhaps puzzled, hesitated, then rushed into the kitchen.

I had to be careful in opening that door in two ways; first, I wanted to look an innocent professional man for as long as possible, and second, I did not want to be shot behind the ear.

Carefully, I opened the door and stood half behind it, looking round at the caller, who stood quite five feet away and off the doorstep. An opening this way enabled me to have a hand in my pocket and on the gun without it being spotted from outside.

'Yes?' I said.

'Who is it?' called Freddie.

'Mr Blake?' asked the man, grinning a little uncertainly.

'All right. It's for me,' I called back, then looked at him.

Though the glimpse had been brief, I recognised the renowned acrobatic stunt man and snatcher of unconsidered trifles.

'I have a message,' he said, still trying to grin.

'Good. What?'

'I should explain,' he said. 'I don't know who it's from. It happened as I was walking along the cliff outside here. A man came up from out of the hedge, though I didn't see anybody hiding there. He stopped me and said, "I want you to take a message to Mr Blake in that house".

'I said right.'

'You said right. Just like that? Without asking what he was doing, who he was?'

'He had a shotgun stuck up my nose. I never ask questions under threat.'

'Go on.'

'He said, "Tell Mr Blake and his women to keep their heads and stay shut in the house tonight. If they don't, they'll get their heads blown off". That's all,' he ended, almost apologetically.

He looked round into the shadows of the trees behind him which overhung the hedge and the cliff path. He looked as if he suspected the shotgun man was still hiding there.

'Well, that's it,' he said. 'I'll be off now.'

'Thank you, Percy,' I said.

He looked surprised for a moment on hearing his name, but shrugged, turned to the gate to the cliff path and went.

I did not look into the shadows around the

house but closed the doors and went back into the kitchen.

2

I made my explanation of the situation short. Neither Freddie nor Laura was surprised, but both seemed angry. Poxon sat back in her chair and regarded us all, one after the other with cold speculation.

'What is this—a den of crooks or something? What's going on? What do you mean, cut off in here till morning?'

'You remember what happened at Tregarrok some months back,' I said. 'It seems that criminal interest in the pile isn't dead yet. That's all.'

'What happens if I go out?' she said aggressively.

'You get shot,' I said simply.

'But I'm nothing to do with any goings-on in this damn place!'

'Explain that, just before you get shot,' I said.

'I'm fuming!' she said explosively.

'We can see it coming out of your ears,' said Laura.

'You shut up!' said Poxon. 'Where's the phone?'

'It's in the next room,' Freddie said. 'Though I can't think why anybody should want to stop our earth and then leave a phone line out.'

Poxon stood up sharply, bouncing with indignation.

'I'll try,' she said, and marched out to find it for herself.

Freddie looked at me.

'It's not aggro all over again is it?'

'It's a leftover from The Death Pit.'

She made a face and turned away.

'I thought we were over all that,' she said.

'So it should have been over,' I said. 'But some people think there was something left.'

'Do you know anything for certain?'

'About who, you mean? No. It's one of these situations where all the people we know about are dead...'

'Don't keep on about it!' she cried out suddenly.

'Leave her,' said Laura. 'Have more beer.' She poured some.

Poxon came marching back.

'Somebody's answering,' she said angrily. 'You should have heard him! Vulgarity! I was speechless. I mean, spoken to like that by a stranger...'

She dropped into a chair.

'Somebody's got the other end outside?' I said.

'Sounds like it,' she said. She was a practical person and next asked, 'Have you got a spare bed? I need sleep. I get crow's feet and I've a lot of work on hand tomorrow.'

Freddie turned back, recovered from her emotion.

'Plenty of beds. It's a question of who'll feel like sleeping.'

'I'll feel like it. Keeping awake ineffectually is merely wasting energy and tautness that might be more useful next day.'

'What's with all this philosophy?' said Laura. 'We are in a mess and if we try and get out of it we get shot. That's how I understand it. Am I wrong?'

'Right,' I said. 'And where a party is prevented from getting out it's always wise to ensure that nobody gets in.' I looked at Freddie.

She nodded. I went first to the washroom off the kitchen and double-bolted the outer door, then through to the front door where I did the same. There were internal shutters on the windows facing the sea winds. I closed those and put the bars across.

That done, I went upstairs. No lights were on up there and there was a sort of grey gloom everywhere as of a moon trying to peer through a new ceiling of clouds. It had been a warm day and some of the upstairs casements were open.

There was a window on the landing above the front door. I leant out and had a look at the scene to the southeast. Ahead were the trees which gathered over the gate to the cliffs, with a few bushes around them leading to the stone hedge.

I could see along the hedge as far as the

distant trees fringing the combe. There was no sign of anyone on that path, and I concentrated on the vegetation by the gate.

It sometimes happens that a threat such as we had had, was meant to give the impression of a considerable armed force surrounding the house.

In fact, two men at opposite corners of the house was enough. That is usual, because each man can cover two house walls.

Sometimes it is a bluff, and there is only one man set to fire whenever he hears anything suspicious. This always keeps people quiet.

I saw nothing suspicious out there, and went through to a bedroom which had a window looking out over the field which ran away to the road. On the right loomed the pile of the great house lurking, almost like some monster Sphinx behind a dwarfed line of trees.

The filtered light picked out everything in dead black and deep grey, contrasting trees and grass and the great house with quite sharp clarity.

It was in this clarity that I saw a man going towards the house from the farm field. He was heading for the hedge boundary at quite a fast pace, but not running.

He was too far away for any identification, but when he got to the stone hedge he took a side run and cleared it with practised ease.

Percy, I thought, was a stunt man who acted in films. The part of calling at the door downstairs and acting the part of a frightened man was not a difficult one.

From the look of the leap into the lions' garden it looked as if he was in with the expected London gang. But then, a hardened, experienced gang does not take on virtuosos who leap balconies and come back to clear the tables, thus creating a furore and the maximum publicity. One thing crooks at work don't like is publicity. It creates too much interest in them and their doings.

If Percy was only then departing, leaving gunmen at the farmhouse, then he was with them.

If he was not with them, then there might not be anyone below at all, but finding out whether there was or not entailed an experiment which might be costly.

I moved on into a spare room at the back of the house. It looked over the long range of cowsheds, joined to a more solidly roofed building below. The sheds were corrugated-iron roofed; the one below the window was an old stone, pitched roof.

By leaning right out of the window I could see to the cliff and the farm hedge bordering it. I thought no one was there, to left or right of that window, so if any guard was there he must be hidden beneath the line of roofs below me.

I have never had a liking for being shut in, specially if it puts me at a disadvantage, and that persuaded me that a risk might pay off.

In any case, the risk of trying to run along the top of a line of pitched roofs seemed greater than the chance that a man might get a shot in at me.

I would be a difficult target, and the marksman might even be momentarily arrested by the lunacy of the effort and not fire at all.

As I thought of it, so I wanted to do it.

My feet could reach the ridge covering without having to drop and possibly lose my footing at the start. I got out of the window and lowered my feet on to it, while still keeping firm hold on the sill.

Part of our business establishment contains a gymnasium for tired businessmen to keep fit, and I have always kept up to scratch in there; ability to make gymnastic moves sometimes being of great use when being pursued by an armed bear during the exit.

I was feeling very impatient then and angry. So far in that visit there had been an atmosphere of having been pursued by the man who wasn't there.

The dead man on the farm; the threatening atmosphere in the big house; the call of the stunt man; Congle's attitude of not knowing what he ought to do to save his skin comfortably; the continued threat of somebody coming who hadn't appeared—and might not appear—all gave the feeling of punching a mattress. One gets exhausted but the mattress stays the same.

Also, I get very impatient, which is the worst fault one can have and survive in the sort of business in which I was then engaged.

I knew all these disadvantages, but if I got out and hurried along that roof I would be behind the enemy, unconfined and with a revolver I was fully able to use effectively.

Three points to me, so I went, without trying to guess how many points there might be to Them.

One thinks such things while engaged in brief manoeuvres, such as dropping gently on to the ridge of the roof below me.

I reached it, pulled the gun out and held it firmly in my right hand, then got my balance.

My idea of getting as far as I could along the roofs was that if anyone was below, he was likely to be close to the house.

There was a grumbling low from a cow who seemed to be ambling around by the sheds ahead of me. It startled me for a moment, for I thought the herd was out on the far side of the field, where I could see some lying on the grass.

The cow's meandering roused a pig, who started grunting noisily. Then another pig joined in and I heard several of them crunching in the straw in the sty. The noise was getting quite animated, which I thought was lucky, as it would attract the attention of anyone there while I made the high wire walk.

I started it then, balancing precariously on

the ridge and moving fairly quickly, step by step, because if I slowed I knew I should fall over.

Then as the grunting got louder I saw a figure go out from near the house to look towards the sty, obviously wondering why the animals were disturbed.

My foot slipped. I knew I was going to go then, no matter what I did, so I threw my weight towards the side on which the man was walking forward, his back then turned to me.

He was foreshortened in my view and I thought I must miss him and fall to the ground behind him if I just let myself go as I was.

So on the way towards the bottom of the slope I took a short leap with one foot from the gutter which gave me just enough forward velocity to land right on his shoulders.

He went down to the ground with me on top. The only noise he made was a terrible grunt, louder than the pigs made.

I scrambled up ready to deal with him, but he needed no dealing.

There was a shotgun under him. The muzzle had stuck into the ground and as he had fallen on it the butt had driven up right into his middle. I winced at the thought of it and turned him over on to his back. He lay quite still.

I looked around, but apart from the cow, who seemed quite uninterested in the human fracas close by, there was no one about.

The man lying there in the light might attract

attention later, so I lugged him into an open shed, then went out and began to creep round the house. I looked carefully into every shadow and saw no one.

But as I came to the front and got a side view of the cliff path I saw Poxon walking away from it down the path towards the combe.

CHAPTER SEVEN

1

Poxon was an independent business woman, very angry about the course events had taken. She had expressed her short tempered view of the whole thing while in the farmhouse, and yet it seemed strange that she should risk being shot by leaving the safety of the house to vent her temper.

She had not seemed irresponsible, and I could not think why the others should have let her go. After all, Freddie had known the sort of mayhem that had gone on in the locality, and Laura had already seen a dead man that day.

They would have believed the danger was real and surely would not have let Poxon go.

The woman went out of sight on the curving, downward path near the trees. I continued my prowl around the house, carefully, necessarily, but saw no one. I went as far as the field hedge to look into the grounds of the Hulk, but there was no movement there either. Percy—if Percy it had been—had melted into the grey black scenery.

The night was quiet. The animals back in the sties had settled down again, and the cows were too far off across the field to be heard ruminating.

The sea had been quiet and calm that day and the idea occurred that in such conditions landing a boat on the difficult beach down in the cove would be easy given the tide right.

I suppose it was the connection between thinking of the calm sea and of the boat stuck up on the gates of Tregarrok. I had no other reason to think of a sea landing.

The upper cloud was thinning then and the moonlight was stronger as I went back to the farmhouse and banged on the door. I heard the dogs bark and then Freddie demand, 'Who's there?'

When I told her, the bolts rattled, the lock clacked with comfortable solidness and she opened the door.

'Why did you let Poxon out?' I said, and went in.

As she closed the door I could see into the kitchen and Poxon was there in her bursting, pinned-up shirt, looking towards me to see who the caller was. She relaxed when she saw. So did Laura.

'You never know who it might be these days,' Poxon said.

Freddie looked askance at me. I took her by

the elbow and we went into the kitchen.

'How did you come in when you didn't go out?' said Laura.

'I got out on to the shed roofs. There was a man on guard but he isn't now. There is nobody else.'

'Then why wait? I'll go,' said Poxon.

'You just went,' I said. 'It looked like you, same slacks, shirt, hair, walking the same way—just like you.'

'Just now?' she said, startled.

'Walking away along the cliff path down towards the combe. I felt certain it was you. So it was somebody deliberately got up like you, same clothes, walk, everything.'

'Deliberately?'

'It was too good to be an accident. Or have you a twin?'

'I am me. My brother is in Venezuela, oiling.'

'Then someone finds you useful,' I said. 'I could understand it if impersonation was used at your boatyard, to get in without being questioned for some reason—but why here, when you're here anyway? Why impersonate when you may come face to face with your original?'

'That is curious,' Poxon said, frowning.

'It's plain barmy,' said Laura.

'The thing is,' said Freddie, 'who is it misleading?'

'It could have misled me,' I said, 'But there

wasn't time between my getting out of the window upstairs and me seeing the lady performing for her to dress up, even if she had the identical clothes handy.'

'They might not have been quite the same,' said Laura. 'It's moonlight out there. Could be a different colour.'

'That still leaves the rest of the imitation.'

'You only saw her from the back?' said Poxon.

'Yes. Walking away at some distance but quite clear. I thought it was you. Can you think of anyone who would act this way?'

'I can't. I suppose it's a decoy somehow, but who would I mislead? What have I got I don't know about? I'm partner in a good business, but it's small, and like the rest, we get good years and years of nervous strain and bank in-fighting. There isn't anything there to attract anybody who wants money for nothing.'

'But you might know somebody they want to know,' I said.

'You mean somebody with money?' she said, cocking her head. 'Let's think. The only people I know with money are customers and we don't have them often. Besides which, I don't get intimate with customers. It gives them the idea they needn't pay for work. Can you imagine?'

'Yes, I can imagine,' said Laura. 'Where I

work it's all like that. So everybody asks for money first.'

'Of course, I don't know your line of business,' said Poxon, quietly insulting.

Freddie held her sister by grabbing her arms from behind. This did not stop the aggrieved one from shouting some short abusive terms.

'And who tipped you off about the boat, anyway?' Laura ended. 'Not another woman, was it?'

'It was the agent for the house. He doesn't want the only entrance blocked up, he says.'

'Not Mr Congle?' said Freddie.

'No. Mr Haigh.'

'Mr Congle tells me he is afraid of what may happen in that house,' I said.

'Who isn't?' said Freddie.

'What did he say?' Poxon asked sharply.

'He said he knew of a London gang who were due to come here and ransack the place. They think there is hidden treasure?'

'I say. That's a bit boys' stuff, isn't it?' said Laura, eagerly.

'Well, this treasure is loot stolen from a series of bank robberies, not pieces of eight.'

'Is there really a lot of it?'

'They think there must be.'

'Then why don't we have a go?' said Laura.

'You'd be the first to be shot,' said Freddie sharply. 'Shut up. If Congle knows someone is coming, then judging from what happened here already, they've arrived!'

'In which case, Laura, do you think your friend Percy is one of them?'

'Percy?' she said surprised. 'Oh no, I...'

'Well?' I said after waiting for her to go on.

'I'm not sure,' she said. 'Taking risks is his business, but from what I hear of these town gangs it would be like riding on a tiger, and he likes risks he can plan a way out of. I don't know, really, if he would or not.'

'Then he might have got wind of it and come down on his own to try it?'

'I should think that's more like it,' Laura said. 'He'd take a risk on his own.'

'But there was another man with a gun outside here,' I said. 'Which suggests they might be together.'

'Or the man might have put him up to warning you,' said Laura. 'By pointing the gun at him while he did it.'

'That's a good reason,' said Poxon.

The way she said it made me think she would be glad to see Percy left out of the suspicions going round, which brought with it the idea she might know him.

I turned my attention back to the old fireplace and the unofficial sweep.

'May I use your lantern?' I said.

Freddie went to the dresser, fetched it and handed it to me. I directed the bright beam on the back of the fireplace above the cooker. It looked a plain stone wall.

From one end of the cooker a vertical flue

stood up and entered the lintel of the chimney breast about a foot and a half back from the front space.

In that underside of the lintel there was an iron soot door. It was black but clean, but the rest of the alcove and the cooker were all clean like the rest of the room as we had found it.

I slid the soot trap door to one side in its guide rails. No soot fell out of the opening revealed.

'What is it?' Laura asked.

'A hole into the flue,' I said, 'where you get the soot out when it gets too thick . . .' I shone the lantern beam into the sooty blackness. There were a few streams of grey heat floating by from the cooker fire and on the left of the opening was something that looked like a fallen brick.

I took up the heavy tool used for removing the ashpan from under the fire, poked it into the hole and moved the brick towards me with the crooked end of the instrument.

When it was about to overbalance and fall, I dropped the tool on the stove top and pulled the object clear with my hand. It was heavy, but it wasn't a brick.

It was a box, a heavy metal box with a hinged lid. I put it on the table and looked at it very carefully.

'Well, open it,' said Laura impatiently.

'We don't know what it is yet,' I said.

In my pocket I had an instrument which

would sniff out whether the box contained explosive of any sort, but to bring it out was to reveal something I had said all along I was not.

Therefore I hesitated, looking at the box.

'For heaven's sake!' said Poxon. She snatched up the box and opened it but suddenly realised what I was afraid of and dropped it. Thus the box smashed wide open as it fell upside down and a shower of jewellery was tumbled out from under it.

'Well, well!' said Freddie. 'Fortune at last!'

Poxon stared down, then bent and picked the whole lot up, box in one hand and jewels in the other. She straightened with her right hand drooling sparkling necklaces like flexible stalactites.

She put it all on the table and the two girls gathered round as if choosing which they should have.

I looked at Poxon because she had a curious attitude of the head as she considered the jewels. Then she looked up at me.

'Imitation,' she said. 'I smell 'em.'

'Are you sure?'

She took a necklace and held it up against the light and for more than a minute she examined each stone with great care. Then she turned and dropped the thing back on the table.

'Dead sure. Its a fake,' she said. 'But it is a copy, I'm sure of that.'

'What sort of copy?' said Laura, disappointed.

'A copy of a very valuable piece indeed,' said Poxon. 'Before you start suspecting me, my father was a jeweller and I was in his business before I married and fell into boats.'

'Why on earth should anybody hide a lot of fakes up my chimney and then clean out the whole kitchen to hide the fact?' said Freddie.

'P'raps he didn't know they were fakes,' said Laura.

'And there are such things as decoy ducks,' I said. 'And this has the appearance.'

'Then what's it hiding?' said Laura.

'Decoys don't hide, they attract,' said Poxon.

2

'I should have thought there was enough attraction round here without laying more traps,' said Laura. 'Already the whole district is creaking with loot, almost sinking into the ground with the weight of the proceeds of sin, so the story goes. Why bother about a box stuck up a chimney?'

'She talks sense,' said Freddie. 'After all, why hide the little box with fakes in it? If they were real then I could understand it.'

'But nobody knows where the main part of the stuff is,' I said, 'that's if it's there at all. A gang of criminals believes that it is there—or they have been led to believe that the whole of the loot was not found after the last sad business.'

'How long has the boat been there?' said Poxon, and answered herself. 'Too long. When the man stuck it there it was because he fancied the criminals were on their way down. But no gang has shown up, has it? So far there has been a friend of Laura's and a man outside this house. That's not a gang.'

'Percy wouldn't be in a gang, I'm sure now,' said Laura quickly. 'He's just not a party man. He likes to be alone. Besides which, I don't think a serious crook would like his sense of humour.'

'So there's no gang,' said Poxon, quite determinedly.

As far as we knew that was true. We were expecting something that hadn't arrived, because I believed that such men as we had envisaged wouldn't be hiding. It was a waste of time. A powerful gang addicted to putting enemies in concrete mixers would not hang about in a dark corner because of three women and a suspected detective.

Therefore, I thought they hadn't come yet, and it was really hard to think why, because the longer you leave such things, the greater the danger that somebody else will find out what you have in mind and cut in first.

Poxon seemed to think along the same lines.

'If you don't think there's a fox,' she said, 'go and repair the wire netting. Why don't we go and look around that old hulk of a house?

We've got lanterns. You have guns, which I have seen in your office. You have, I suppose, got shot for them, being a farmer. Right. We are prepared. Here we are sitting in a chicken run thinking there isn't a fox. Best to go out and see.'

'I'm all for it,' said Freddie slowly, even warily, 'but why are you?'

'Somebody imitated me,' said Poxon. 'So I am marked. With a decoy stuffed up the chimney, we are all marked. Surely Mr Blake will agree with me?'

'Certainly,' I said. 'But I think you don't know that house.'

'Tell me about it,' said Poxon.

'It's a labyrinth. A maze. One could be lost in there for quite a time. There are no plans. The whole building, patched together by different people, with different notions, over centuries, could defy a jungle hunter. It is dark—not that daylight helps much. There could be a gang going into the place.'

'They could be as lost as we are,' said Freddie. 'Why not?'

'I'd sooner be moving than stay here,' said Laura, with a touch of petulance. 'I'd sooner be shot at in the dark by somebody as blind as me than in here where he can see me and I can't him.'

I laughed then. It was humorous to think of these three going on a night hunt for London crooks who might well be nonplussed by such a collection of amateurs all in disagreement with each other.

On the other hand, one can confuse an expert so that he has to waste precious moments wondering whether he has strolled into a lunatic asylum in error for a bank.

As we stood, we were, at best, in a small fort, and, militarily, forts besieged have to wait for relief. I would never stay in a fort but I would no more dodge out of one with a baggage of three, all at war with one another.

It seemed, though, that the only thing to do was to go with them. It was a hard life when I had come expecting only one woman, to find the wrong one, then a wrong second, and the right one only in time to make up a trio. But it had happened and I could see no way of disbanding without, perhaps getting them shot in the farmhouse.

On the other hand, they might as well get shot in the dark house, or anywhere on the way to it...

If the gang had arrived.

There was evidence at that stage of four men only; the dead one at the old farm, the amateur sweep, Percy and the man out by the milking sheds. That could boil down to three if the gunman had been doubling as the sweep.

Just who the decoy was meant to attract was difficult to see without knowing what gang, or other persons intended to come to Tregarrok.

A horrid thought struck me that it might

have been meant for Jonathan Blake, in which case, it meant they knew who I really was.

The idea that the opposition might have known that, and what I was to do there, before the visit started at all, put a new view on the situation.

So far no gang had turned up to walk into a trap, for that was what it was intended to be, and it was an interesting thought that, if the snare had been spotted at the very outset, it might have been re-set as a trap to get me.

I had no idea why any London gang should be so interested in me except that, somehow, they had found out about the police waiting roundabouts.

If that was the case, then I suspected Congle at once.

But the trouble with Congle was his insatiable greed. He would never share anything, specially not with people who, at best, would let him have only a small percentage of the proceeds.

If, then Congle was helping somebody, it was initially for his own personal gain; in short, he meant to do them down after he had got them to do as much dirty work as he needed. That was Congle, as I knew well by then.

He had just come out of jail where he had heard, he said, about the attempt to find more loot. He could well have done so, and anything he had heard he would certainly have turned to his own advantage.

It seemed to me then that perhaps the most sensible thing to do was to leave the farmhouse—with the harem, because my attachment to them seemed unbreakable then—and go to Congle's farm.

But, as he had already seen me in Tregarrok, he might well have decided not to be at his farm in case I called.

Laura interrupted.

'Well, are we going? I mean, if there really is some treasure lying about, let's get at it. I don't mind dying rich.'

'Let's get out of here,' said Poxon sharply. 'I don't like that fake stuff in the box. Something's due to happen here, I feel, and the sooner I'm away from it the better off I'll be.'

I picked up the box, put the stuff in it as before, then shut it and put it back in its hidey hole in the flue. I pushed the sliding trap across. Not a grain of soot fell.

'All right,' I said. 'You'd better get the shotguns. And make sure they work.'

'They work,' said Freddie and went out of the kitchen.

The three of us followed. I came last and snicked the kitchen light off. There was not then a light on anywhere in the house, but the moonglow seemed quite light outside.

'What about the dogs?' Freddie said.

'We'll have them with us to the house. They'll know if anyone's hiding on the way. When we get there, send them to cover to wait.

All right?'

'Right,' Freddie said.

She got a big torch and a lantern. The two guns were in working order. She made sure of that and also pocketed some rounds of cartridges in the leather jacket she put on. Laura took the second gun.

Poxon took no notice of these proceedings, for she was at the window near the main door, peering out almost as if expecting to see somebody outside.

The dogs kept quiet all the time, watching Freddie as if they knew something was very wrong.

When she had satisfied herself about the guns and the lamps, she spoke a single word to the setters.

'Heel,' she said.

I imagine this meant quiet as well, as if they were poacher's dogs trained to a whisper.

For some reason Poxon wanted to go out first, but I persuaded her to stand back. She did not complain about having no weapon but Freddie shoved a shooting stick in her hand.

'You can stab them with one end and whack them with the other like a bat,' she said.

'I don't propose to fight anybody,' Poxon said. 'I'm just jagged at the edges from being cooped in here. If I can get through that house and out to my vehicle that's the way I'm going.'

I opened the door. Freddie signalled the dogs to come up to me, and they did, like a couple of ghosts. It was quiet everywhere out there, just the faint hiss and murmur of the sea down on the shingle beach.

I went out on the grass beside the path. The dogs followed very alert, very watchful, searching the air for any scent of a stranger, but clearly found none.

The others followed as quietly as the dogs. The light was not bright but it was several points above plain dark, and as we had the dogs' noses, I would have preferred almost darkness.

We kept a tattered formation, and as we came into the edge of the copse which ran up to the higher part of the big house grounds, I left the women, went back and took a look at the gunman.

He was still out—he had taken my full weight so that wasn't surprising—but I took a precaution of doing him up with binder twine in case he did wake up with bad feelings.

I then took the shotgun, which I should have done before, but as I had stuffed it behind an old manger I hadn't left it very handy.

The women were waiting in the copse. Apart from them there was no sign of anyone about. The dogs watched me, standing quite still to make sure with a silent sniff of the air towards me there was no mistake on their part.

When I rejoined them it was still Poxon who was impatient to go.

'Let's get to this house. It seems naked out

here,' she said.

'What's *your* hurry?' Laura said, as if suddenly realising something.

Poxon looked back from the act of going on ahead.

'I want to be shot of this damn place,' she said. 'I told you that. It's getting on my nerves. I want into my car and out. Just like that.'

She turned and went on. Laura went after her as Freddie and I turned to go on to the house.

'What are you up to?' said Laura belligently.

'Don't be childish!' snapped Poxon, without looking round.

She was marching ahead then towards the house, and Laura was close behind, so we had to catch up as well. The dogs followed but I noticed the English Setter began to appear uneasy. Twice he stopped, pointed and sniffed towards the shrubbery by the end of the great house which was then on the left of our heading.

The Irish Setter began to take the same notice and Freddie slowed down.

'Somebody in the shrubs,' she whispered.

'Keep on to the corner,' I said. 'Keep the dogs with you. I'll go back when we get there. Once round the corner, stop them all in the shelter of that garden wall. Right?'

'Right.'

We went on. She hissed to the dogs, and they followed her obediently, though clearly their interest was fixed in that shrubbery.

We reached the corner of the great building. To the left the wall ran down to the shrubbery with a few small trees lining the path alongside the house.

We all went into the shelter of the house corner and the garden wall which, ten feet along from the corner, jutted out from it.

One of the dogs went 'Wuff!' Freddie hissed it quiet.

That was a mistake.

CHAPTER EIGHT

Obediently the dog made no more sound. In the grey light I saw Poxon watching me instead of peering round to spot the menace of someone hiding perhaps to ambush us.

Poxon was an increasing mystery. She had expressed an anxiety to get away as quickly as possible—but by going through Tregarrok house, with every danger that might have, and reaching her own car at the jammed gates.

But there had been two vehicles by the side of the farmhouse; my car and Freddie's pickup, and she had not suggested we use either of those in order to get her out.

She was, after all, the only one of the four who lived elsewhere that night and hadn't expected to be staying in this locality at all.

And somebody out on the cliff had taken the trouble to impersonate her, so whatever else she might be, she was known, for some reason, by someone who was in that area for no good reason.

That, again, had been puzzling, in that there seemed to be no sensible answer as to which watcher in the dark had been the intended victim of the charade.

I was out of the farmhouse, but nobody could have seen me get out of the back, drop on the gunman and then come round the house, and have dressed up as Poxon while those few seconds passed.

That impersonation must have meant earlier preparation. It also might have meant that it was designed, not so much for the promenade on the clifftop but for some later double act, perhaps to prove an alibi.

If that was the case then Poxon was very much concerned with the expected crime at the dark house. Certainly her real business was with the stranded boat, but it could also be a very convenient stranding.

Which gave me to think about Laura's boyfriend from whom she had won the boat. He had jammed it on the gates as a result of which Poxon had turned up—but only after quite a while.

I thought of these things while watching the bushes and little trees where the dogs had sensed somebody hiding. The women were in the angle of the jutting wall behind me.

'Can you see anybody?' Freddie said in a whisper.

'Is the dog still uneasy?' I said.

'Tense. It's still in the bushes, whatever is hiding there.'

The stillness amongst the bushes seemed to indicate that the hiding man knew he had been spotted and kept quite still to try and convince us he wasn't there after all.

To go on into the house leaving a sentinel who knew we were in there would be to seal our fate in more ways than one. He could tip off his masters, or sell his information, or at the least, block our way of escape.

I felt it best to take a risk and draw him out than leave him there.

I whispered to Freddie.

'When I signal, send the dogs over to the wall and make them stay the other side. Right?'

She nodded. The dogs were very well trained.

I peered round the corner of the house down to the thicket and the bushes further along. There was no movement. The man the dogs had scented there was lying very low, hardly breathing, I would have said.

I held up a finger, and ran out and along towards the bushes, my borrowed gun at the ready. Behind me the dogs flashed out, the white setter showing up splendidly as they made their diversionary run towards the stone wall boundary of the farm.

They made some row at the same time, barking excitedly, and there was no doubt that anyone watching in the bushes would have his attention split by that performance.

I ran fast to match with the diagonal track of the dogs and reached the edge of the thicket. The clump had grown up against the house wall, seeded there wild and never cut down. It was a tangled mass of bushes and small trees grown across the path and the only way to the other side seemed to be round the outside.

Going round it with a man inside it would defeat the purpose of my being there, which was to find the man and stay alive at the same time.

The growth was not that thick in May but by that light it was bewildering as I peered through the maze of twigs, thorns and young leaves.

The dogs did a final leap over the stone wall and then were heard no more as they obeyed instructions and waited behind it.

I seemed to see a darker shadow against the house wall; but it was so indistinct I could not be sure it was a man or a bush.

I said, 'Percy, what are you doing now?'

The shadow moved with a sudden jerk.

'I've got a gun on you, Percy,' I said. 'So don't risk aiming at me.'

There was a sudden rustle and screech of twigs against the wall and the uncertain shadow moved very suddenly to one side away from me and went out of sight behind a thicker barrier of leaves.

I ran quickly round the outside of the thicket, keeping careful watch in amongst the little trees. I saw a shadow, like a fast moving man, show up against the house wall for an instant in a break in the leaves, and then he seemed to leap upwards.

For a moment it looked as if he had turned into a human spider. He scaled the wall and vanished as if he had gone into thin air leaving the great wall intact.

From that moment there was silence and the foliage stopped shivering from the running man's passage.

I found a way into the wild little wood and got through to the house wall, which ran up to a dizzy height like a great grey cliff with an unbroken face.

But of course, it couldn't be. The man had got into it somewhere, so there must be an opening there on the lines of the other trick doorways in that monstrosity of a house.

In that light I could not make out any consecutive lines that might make an opening, for the whole wall was a patchwork of local stone of all shapes and sizes and could have concealed a half dozen openings without showing amongst the ragbag of joints.

From the swiftness of his response to my call and his vertical climb I felt sure I had been right in guessing it was Percy. If so, what was he doing there?

As a guard he had been a bad one; he had guarded nothing and fled at the sight of the opposition. He might go in somewhere and say we were at the house, something which would have been suspected before a guard was set anyway. He should have been there to watch and see what we were doing, and he hadn't stayed for that.

Therefore, I guessed, he was still by himself.

Then why watch us? Loners usually get on with the job, glancing over their shoulder now and again. Because they are on their own they can work very fast; there is no one to do something wrong, and no one to give them away.

Yet here was Percy, performing tricks on the cliff edge, shinning up blank walls like a spider and apparently getting nowhere, because while he was doing all that he wasn't looking for treasure.

I went on through the scratchy thicket until I broke out of it and went round the back of that great wing of the house to the old kitchens, where I knew my way.

It was just possible that, by working my way up to the next floor from the kitchen I might find the opening he had got in by. I wanted to get in touch with him to find out if he was by himself or with a gang.

In which case he would know who they were,

and to find that out was my main purpose in being there.

I went in at the back where the door had long since been unhinged and used for firewood. It was leaving the women outside—I hoped—but if I met Percy I wanted to see him quite away from the Lawrence sisters, Freddie and Laura.

I went through the kitchens up to the old staff stairs—or one of the many—which should lead against the wall through which Percy had so magically disappeared. When I got to the top of them there was a window which showed a glow of grey light inside and indicated a door at the top of the stairs. I went to it and opened it very carefully, because, if the window was the only light this side or the other, I might present a vague target to any interested person.

Nothing happened. Looking past the edge of the solid old door I saw a line of five such windows on the wall ahead of me.

No curtains were drawn—perhaps they would have fallen apart if anyone had tried it. Certainly the dirt on the panes made the grey light dim, just enough to see block shapes and little else.

I went through the doorway into the passage. The direction of it must, I knew, crank to the left to get to the central feature of the great hall or otherwise come to a dead end.

I went along carefully and saw no opening in the wall where the windows were, no place where the human spider could have got through. As there was none in the kitchen either, as I already knew, then the secret entry must be between the floors.

Such a way in might come up—or down anywhere; up through a bedroom floor, down through a store room ceiling, so it would be a waste of time looking further for it.

Designed to cheat the excise men and other lawful investigators, the puzzles of the great house were even at this day, not out of date.

I went on to the expected turn in the corridor into another wide passage where there was a slightly better light at the end, so I guessed it led on to the gallery round the great hall.

I saw a shadow a few yards ahead of me, moving very slowly, almost meandering. It was a tall figure, but I had an idea it was that of a woman, perhaps because of the slow, almost idling sort of walk.

Perhaps she was waiting, so it was as well for me to expect another person to turn up from in front of her or behind me.

In that case it might be better not to wait, so I went ahead quickly, being as quiet as I could, but in conditions of cathedral silence, being so quiet as not to be heard is impossible, so I made it fast.

She turned suddenly, just as I got to her.

'Don't say anything.' I spoke very quietly and pushed the gun muzzle into her tummy to show I was not suggesting quiet, but advising it for her own good.

'Oh dear,' she breathed, almost with a relieved sound. 'It must be Mr Blake. I've been so wanting to meet you.'

The light was dim, but from the action, the voice and the pinned shirt and slacks I was sure I had got Poxon's double.

The only thing about her was that, but for her saying she had not met me, she was exactly like Poxon, moving, shaping and talking.

It did not seem so much a disguise job as a genuine twin set.

'Who are you waiting for?' I said.

'My sister.'

'Poxon?'

'Whoever's Poxon?'

'I thought you said your sister.'

'Yes.'

'Then what is your name and hers?'

'Fairlane. We're both Fairlane.'

'That's the name of the boat jammed on the gates?'

'Of course. That's what we've come about. It's my boat.'

One finds all sorts of crazy people, particularly those found wandering in deserted hulks of houses may be suspected of brain tremors, but I was not quite sure then which of the two of us was barmy.

'But it's supposed to have been won by a girl here as a gambling debt.'

'So it was, but when she won it, she didn't

know the man betting it didn't own it.'

'She doesn't now, either.'

'And it is awkward because the thing's stuck on the gate. I'm sure Alan did it deliberately so we couldn't get it back.'

'Have you got a boatyard in Mar?'

'In Mar? Where's that?'

I told her and she shook her head.

'We've got a boatyard but it's right away along the coast at Shoreham, Sussex.'

I was utterly confused by what possible reasons could have made Poxon tell stories which had part truth, but in the wrong geographical places, and outright lies about the right places. But perhaps she was a compulsive yarner and loved spinning tales to kid people.

But why had she pretended she hadn't known her twin sister was out on the cliff?

'Did you come down here with her—Poxon, we call her?'

'We came together, yes, but I went off to see what haulage machinery we could hire to get the boat off those gates. She said she'd call at the farmhouse because that was where the girl was who thought the boat was hers.'

The idea that this sister, too, might be a wanderer from the truth faded a little, because that short explanation hung together.

'Did you arrange to meet her in here?'

'She said in that big hall place downstairs. I'm just looking round—or I was. I'm now trying to find my way back to where I started.'

‘Did you hear anyone come in up here, about fifteen minutes ago?’

‘No. I should probably have screamed. This place is worse than the Chamber of Horrors.’

‘Weren’t you frightened to come in here?’

‘I wasn’t to start with. Then I thought of rats and bats and ghosts and corpses and all I could think of was to get out quickly, but I kept going down the wrong corridors and couldn’t see enough to know where I was. It was like a nightmare.’

She seemed too genuine to be real, specially for anyone being found in that place and being able to pass it all off so naturally, at the same time making herself look rather slow or stupid; which alone, is a rare performance.

‘Why do you think your sister is pretending to be someone else?’

‘My sister is always pretending. She is the biggest liar you have ever come across, and that isn’t a bet, it’s a fact.’

There again the simple grand slam returning the question, but it takes a smart mind to be simple and direct and to play it precisely that way.

‘Is there anyone else you expected to meet here?’ I asked without making too much of a point of it.

She seemed to think for a minute, but the light was too dim for me to see any expression.

‘I can only speak for myself, and that’s no, but I can’t answer for my sister.’

‘Yet you guessed my name.’

‘A man was here and he told me you were doing a job here in the house.’

‘Who?’

‘Oh, a big, fat, old, waddling, alcoholic bag of humanity who wheezed out his name was—what was it? Something very odd. Bongle? Dongle? No, Congle, I think it was.’

Well, that was on the level, too, because I knew he had been in the house though he had appeared to go faster than he said he had intended.

The place was dead quiet, and I guessed the women were still waiting outside, which was probably better for them if anyone unpleasant did turn up, although by that time I found myself continually wondering just what had happened to cause nothing to happen.

‘Have you seen your sister since you left her by the boat?’

‘No,’ she said. ‘She said to meet her in here, but she’s been hours. I think she’s having trouble convincing the girl.’

‘And you’ve just been wandering about?’

‘Actually I enjoyed myself. It’s a lovely quiet spot, and I love quiet spots.’

‘Haven’t you seen anybody at all apart from Mr Congle?’

‘I saw a man or two wandering about with guns under their arms, but they shoot in the country, don’t they? Rabbits and things.’

I heard a sound somewhere near us and got

hold of her arm as a warning to keep quiet. Her response was excellent, she just hissed very quietly to let her breath out, then stood perfectly still.

The sound did not repeat and I thought that whoever had made it was listening to find out if anyone had heard and been alarmed. We had been talking, very low, indeed, but audible to anyone not so far off, so to encourage the listener to do more I decided it was best to go on talking.

'I think something fell down,' I said.

She let more breath go, as if quite genuinely strained by the tension of listening for someone in the dark.

She said, 'Thank goodness. I thought it was another rat.'

'Let us go on to the hall,' I said. 'It's lighter there.'

I took her elbow and guided her along to the hall gallery, as I thought, but once again the trickery of the disjointed architecture fooled me.

We came on to a gallery, but it looked down into what looked like some kind of dusty museum.

'This isn't where I came in,' she said, and stopped by the railing.

I led her slightly along the gallery so we did not show in the opening of the passage we had just left.

Nothing happened. It seemed that someone

who had been near us in the passage had decided to keep clear, guessing that we knew that the noise we had heard had not been that of something falling down.

I was becoming more puzzled about the whole lack of event in that place. I was sure it had been Percy who had fled into the house from outside when I had challenged; the girls I had left below had been almost eager to come here, yet, if nobody else, Congle had spread it about that a dangerous London gang was due any moment.

I was at Tregarrok because of it and yet here were several quite ordinary people mulling around as if being buried in a concrete road bridge was an end greatly to be desired.

It made no sense at all. In fact, nothing had made sense since I had arrived.

Hiding fakes up a chimney to decoy somebody who would know damn well the real loot wasn't in that cottage anyway, but in the house.

Guarding people in a house with a gunman stationed on the one side of the house where there were no doors at all, and from which position he would not even see one.

True we had thought there were others besides him, but there were not.

Percy the idiot stunt man had behaved normally only once when calling to tell us the farmhouse was surrounded. On the other two occasions he had appeared for the sole purpose of spectacular disappearances, it seemed.

Poxon turned up pretending to be Poxon and painting a broad local scene to go with it, yet her sister who had come with her told a differently placed story, also asserting that the boat was theirs, which tangled things more.

At the very start Congle had pretended not to be in his office, yet had pretty soon turned up at Tregarrok where he knew I was bound to meet him again.

There had to be a single thread tying the lot together, and I had thought it to be the imminent London gang, but to judge by their actions, the rest of the cast didn't believe in it.

Or were they all of a heroic and impatient nature?

That seemed the most unlikely solution to any problem.

I suppose because of the odd behaviour of all these people I began to wonder whether the London gang was a fabric of some tortuous imagination based on some past facts.

Not for the first time I thought it incredible that a gang, knowing the house was vast, in great grounds, in a lonely place and empty, should hang about before searching it. Surely the expected thing was for them to come at once, dispatch anybody who happened to be looking on, grab what they could find and go.

Yet here they were, apparently determined on the raid some days ago, leaving it to wait while a scattered band of armed—if amateur—

guerillas was forming all over the small area.

The farmhouse guard, Percy, the Lawrence sisters and the Fairlane sisters, Congle, Haigh, the dead man at the old farm and perhaps more I hadn't seen or thought of.

Also the young man who had 'lost' the boat and jammed it on the railings must have known of something about to happen or he would not have gone to the trouble of doing the job so thoroughly.

'The man who brought your boat here,' I said quietly. 'Do you know him? Did you hire it to him?'

'Yes. That is, yes, we hired it to him. That's why he couldn't have lost it gambling, you see. He rang us and said there had been an accident and he'd had to dump it here.'

At least that netted several people together by way of the boat; Laura, the gambling young man and Percy, and the Fairlane sisters. Percy being drawn in because he had been at the club with Laura and her gambler, and also he had turned up at Tregarrok.

So it looked like the boat was the link.

I looked down into the museum hall, another of the miracles of deception in the architecture of that house because, as far as one could see from the outside, there was no room for it.

There were cases standing about, chests, human dummies, totem poles—or that's what things looked like in the grey light. But whatever the details, the place was definitely laid out as a museum.

'How did you leave the hall?' I said. 'Up the main stairs?'

'Yes, I went up there and then round to my right. It had rather a soothing atmosphere. That's why I wandered. I am a bit that way. Wandery.'

'Of course, you never had a feeling somebody was near you?'

She shivered.

'Gosh, no! I'd have screamed.'

But she hadn't screamed when I had come up behind her in the corridor.

'I think we'd best go down there,' I said.

She agreed. She seemed to agree to anything.

We went to the stairs, which were quite narrow, and down into the hall. Once down there it did not seem so large as it had when seen from the gallery.

The glass of the cases was thick with dust and some of the draped figures looked as if they were made from cobwebs. Three mummies were standing about outside their cases and looked more horrific than any made-up job for a film, specially in that light.

We noticed something together. I said nothing, but she did.

'Isn't that funny,' she said, 'the floor's not dusty like the rest.'

Non dust areas had been a feature of the house when I had been there before, but the rooms had been entirely free of dust not dusty with only the floor fairly clean.

It looked like a rapid job done very recently to conceal a movement through this hall without letting marks show up like footprints in the snow.

'What a funny thing to do,' she said, stopping and looking round. 'Just dusting the floor and leaving everything about all dirty so the floor will get dirty quicker. It falls down, you know, dust...'

She stopped talking very suddenly, and looked quickly round.

'I'm fey,' she said quickly. 'Do you know that? I'm fey. I can sense when there's something wrong. There's something dead here. Not the mummies. Somebody freshly dead!'

CHAPTER NINE

1

In an unlit hall of mummies late at night, it was understandable that even the strongest nerved might smell death, therefore I did not take Miss Fairlane's shivery remark as seriously as undoubtedly she meant it.

'Can you see anything to give you that idea?' I said.

'I can smell it, I tell you. New death. Not mummies.'

'Keep still.'

I held her arm and looked round the gallery which ran along three walls of the hall museum. There was no movement in the shadows up there.

The grey moonlight was filtering in through the glass of a domed roof, giving a twilight effect, where the mummies and their great empty half cases stood like tombstones in a forgotten churchyard. In such a light, and in such circumstances it seemed all the upright figures watched us.

'I can see nothing but these things,' I said.

'I feel there is a dead man here, somewhere.' She was rigid with fear.

The place was thick with dust except where the paths had been swept through it for someone to go by without showing footprints.

It had to be, therefore, that if a body was left there, it would be somewhere within reach of the broomswept paths.

I took another glance at the gallery, then looked around me and listened, but heard nothing beyond the woman's soft, quick breathing.

There was a possibility that if she were alone, she might be attacked, if she was what she said she was. The only thing about that saying was that she had said she and Poxon had come down together, yet when I mentioned a double on the cliff, Poxon had pretended to be incredulous.

However, Miss Fairlane did seem genuinely disturbed then.

'Stand by this case,' I said, guiding her towards the empty cover of a mummy case. 'It will cover you while I look round.'

There seemed to be dozens of mummies as I left her standing by the case and started my search. In fact, there were six, but three stood free of their cases, which in two parts, provided three standing figures for each one.

To find mummies in such a place was perhaps not so strange, for smuggling was the lore and tradition of Tregarrok, and what better to bring in valuables than in the wrappings of some departed Pharaoh?

I kept a sharp look out in the shadows round me, but the walls below the overhanging galleries were ink black and nothing could be spotted there. I had an advantage in that I was moving amongst the mummies and their boxes and it would be difficult for anyone to be sure which upright shadow was me.

For that reason—to confuse any possible watcher—I kept moving in and out and round the obstacles. It did not matter to me how much dust I trod in so there was no need for me to follow the paths.

Then I came to the front of a sarcophagus, where the human face on the front looked over the swept path. I approached it from its open side and then I saw what Miss Fairlane had meant.

There was a dead man in there, jammed tightly against the sides so that he could not fall out; so he was big and fat and I thought of Congle.

I would not show a light, even my small pea lamp, because it would be such a fine target for any interested party, so I peered into the fallen face as it hung staring to the floor at my feet.

The smell of stale tobacco made it certain this was the doubtful agent who had so recently escaped one law and was now caught by another and worse one.

I managed to make out the bloated features and in doing it, I saw a knife handle sticking out of his waistcoat. It looked a very old-fashioned device, perhaps one taken from the collection of curiosities in that museum.

With Congle dead there seemed to be a clearing of the air, for he had always been a suspect. But it did not give any indication of who had killed him, unless it had been Percy in the course of his restless wanderings.

I looked round me and made very sure there were no live figures standing amongst the long dead, then went back to where I had left the Poxon sister.

She was not there.

I made sure before I looked further around, for she could have got into a mummy case one half or the other, but she hadn't.

During my search I had heard nothing at all, certainly nothing that could have indicated a scuffle, so I assumed that the lady had crept away on her own.

She might have been so frightened she could not stay there with those fearful figures all round her. I could understand that if she had. She had been frightened, as I had noticed from the tone of her voice, and I felt sure that hadn't been faked.

In which case I thought she wouldn't have gone back upstairs because she had heard someone up there. Even if the person up there was known to her, for in that case she would have kept away from him rather than let me know who he was.

So, innocent or guilty, I felt she had gone away by some downstairs exit.

I moved away then and went between the flat cases of assorted curios, mostly invisible because of the dust on the glass, to a position in the deep shadow under the gallery.

It was silent as a tomb, which indeed, it was. The woman's exit had been extraordinarily silent so that I wondered again whether she could still be somewhere by the sarcophagi, except that she would certainly have spoken to me.

I went quickly along under the gallery until I came to a door. When I tried to open it I found it locked. I left it and went on, but remembered that until then I had never found a locked door in all that place of puzzles.

There was no corridor which corresponded

on plan to the one where I had found the woman upstairs, but in this crackpot place that did not matter. But it made me wonder more why that door had been locked, because it was a large door, too large for a cupboard.

I leant my back against the wall and looked around the grey lit scene of the cases and the horror figures of the mummies. In that silence I began to wish that someone would appear and have a go at me.

I wished that because I felt then it would be the quickest way to find out what exactly was going on in that place. What we had expected had not happened. No London gang, no opposition, just the wandering women and the disappearing Percy.

And yet somebody had killed the man at the old farm.

Though nothing violent seemed to have happened here, that certainly had. It made me wonder whether our trap was not too late, that the gang had been and gone, leaving that dead man behind.

Congle's death I did not regard in the same light, for Congle was the sort of man most likely to be rubbed out because somebody didn't like him, and there must have been plenty such somebodies.

Congle was local—but then so was the dead man at the farm. He had worked for Congle at one time. That link had not seemed important until I remembered that some time ago I had seen Congle trying to shoot him.

True, that had been an affaire de coeur with Congle's wife, but the spirit of hatred had been there. Now both were dead.

I did not think the man had acted with Congle this time because of the animosity between them, but the farmworker had been on my land where he had never been before as far as I knew, then had come straight back and been killed.

Now Congle had been killed, but in a different place. So, if the farmworker had been killed because he had found something, and I guessed, so had Congle, they had each found the same thing in different places.

It was an interesting thought because it seemed to mean Congle had surprised his ex-worker with the information, killed him, taken the gen and followed it back to Tregarrok, where he himself had been surprised.

The only information I had in mind was the location of some undiscovered store of loot, yet if the labourer had the information what was he doing at the old farm?

Further, if Congle had killed him for the information, he had been a damn long time putting it to use, for the man had been dead hours, and Congle alive not so long ago.

I went on round the wall under the gallery and found no exit. I retraced my steps to the foot of the staircase and went slowly, very carefully up, holding the shotgun ready. When at eye level with the gallery floor I looked carefully along in each direction, and saw nothing but a pair of suits of armour, one half toppling over.

The light was tricky, and the effect of the partly toppled suit made the other look as if it had begun to move forward and then stopped.

I went up on to the gallery and looked at its return part which ran along the opposite wall—that was the side behind which the great hall should lie.

There seemed to be an opening there but in that light it was difficult to be sure. I decided to try for it rather than the one by which the woman and I had come into this death place.

Perhaps I had the feeling that I should not trust that upright suit of armour. In any case, with one man dead below, it was foolish not to be careful.

As I began to go towards the return of the gallery, there was a grunt, a clanging and a clattering clash that shook the bats out of the high roof. I saw two begin to flap uncertainly about under the glass dome as if startled.

The toppling armour had collapsed entirely. I felt it was a very unusual coincidence that after years of standing lopsidedly there it should have selected this moment to subside altogether.

There was no other sound or movement, but I watched the armour and the opening between them the suits had been guarding.

Something had shifted the old iron enough to make it fall at last; something larger than a bat, who wouldn't have flown into it anyway; bats, having radar, don't hit things.

I kept perfectly still with the gun ready, watching that slit of an opening, but perhaps startled by the sudden fall of the ironwork. Nothing happened for more than a minute.

I realised then that it was going to be that kind of game. Waiting until somebody's nerves give way.

And that was not at all the sort of game the London gangs play.

2

In a waiting game the result usually goes to the one who can keep still longest because that is the hardest thing in the world to do.

There was one advantage I had, and that was to be at the head of the stair, so that whatever happened, I could dodge in three directions, whereas anyone on the floor had only two. Excepting, of course, the bats, which had then wakened up and enticed two more out from their naps or whatever they had been doing.

The tiny flapping of the wings was disconcerting, because in the silence it was very clear and almost loud enough to disturb the earnest listener.

The seconds went by. Nothing happened but that the bats had decided to have a race meeting and were beating about in all directions in the great space of the museum.

I thought they must be just having fun because there were no insects flying about inside that mausoleum; the spiders would not have allowed enough to feed an army of bats, and from the cobwebs about one saw the spiders were in control.

It is good to think of natural history and other creatures while waiting to be shot, because it gives an instant appreciation of the slightest change in the scene, should any take place.

None did, but I kept on. The bats lived up in the roof somewhere so they must have had a way out through it to reach the open air and the hunting grounds of dusk—

Which brought the wandering mind to rest on the possibility that perhaps my enemy had three dimensions; not down through a flight of stairs, but up towards the roof.

If he had dislodged some pieces of old plaster or cement which had fallen, then that could have toppled the old armour quite easily.

And a presence up there would most likely have disturbed the bats.

But for some reason, he could not see me where I stood by the stairhead.

I began to search the shadows of the ceiling beside the light silver bowl of the dome. It was difficult, because the ceiling beside the circle of light was as black as had been the wall beneath the gallery.

My mind sorted out Percy, the stunt man, as being the most obvious person to shin up walls and hide in the rafters amongst the bats, but it could not sort out why I was not shot at, for I must have been partially visible though the stair-rail by me would have confused the scene.

The bats were calming rather and flying much slower, then they began to thin out, as if one by one, going back up into the roof.

That seemed to indicate that whoever was above had left the hall somehow, but I had seen and heard nothing but the flapping bats.

In which case it would be the second time someone had disappeared into a blank wall, and it indicated that the someone knew more than a few tricks about the place.

Such knowledge would take a long time, even with a lucky accident, and several visits. Yet it had been said to me that Percy, the most likely person of agility enough, had never been here before this visit.

Only Laura could have been sure of that, because she knew him and no one else admitted that disaster.

Watching a shadowed area for some time results in one of two effects on the sight; it might clear so that you see what's there, or it might get playful so that you see what isn't.

I began to make out a still shape up against the rafters in the corner of the ceiling almost above the corridor entrance. It looked like a blob. It was motionless and the bats had settled or gone out, apparently no longer uneasy.

The old silence had come again and I went very slowly, and making no noise, along the wall to where the armour had toppled, then looked up to that shadow about eight feet above the lintel of the opening.

And then I saw that it was another opening, like a circular window, but looking on to darkness instead of the grey moonlight.

From that it looked as if there was a passage above the one we had used, and since somebody had just escaped by it, it seemed an even bet this was the trick passage that ran straight to the outside wall, where I had seen the disappearing trick a half hour before.

There were many puzzling features about Tregarrok, but any reason for putting a secret passage above one that was there already escaped me.

An escape way when the customs officers were in the passage below? Yes, but how did one get up to the escape window without a noticeable ladder?

How did one get down the house wall outside, having got to the end of the escape route? Hanging ropes would be obvious, and also the sort of thing the officials would be looking for.

The only sane reason I could see for such a passage was that it led to a secret place which could be got at both from outside and inside.

I felt sure the man who had killed Congle

had got up there while I was actually watching, he had opened the window and got in, dislodging something as he had done so, and that something had fallen and collapsed the old armour suit.

If that were the case, and I could see no other excuse for the internal window, I had best get up there somehow and look for myself.

There were chests in the passage. One stood on end might hoist me high enough to get a hold on the window ledge.

I made a slow appreciation of the museum above and below to see if I could detect a sign of anyone still alive, but the old stillness was complete.

Before I did anything I thought of the Fairlane woman and her swift and silent vanishing; of the three women still, I thought, waiting outside or just in the main hall and I wondered just who else there was left now at Tregarrok.

Haigh, perhaps, and Percy. A man tied up at the farm, and another dead further away. There was the boat gambler who had, it was said, never stayed.

Beyond all doubt there was no gang. There is a certain safety in numbers because numbers make more noise and show where they are.

It seemed likely then that the problem was not the gang—they might come later—but a single, silent, secret murderer who was nearing his goal by killing one man after another, and was in no haste.

The chests were heavy and moving one took time because the work was not quiet, and I paused very often indeed to look all round and be ready to fire if necessary.

No one appeared to take any interest. I got the chest out on to the gallery floor under the passage mouth, then upended it. The rise it gave would leave me still a foot below the window ledge with my arms up.

I clambered up on top of the chest and took a closer look at the old window. It appeared to be improperly closed. I pushed the gun muzzle up and managed to get it behind the closing edge. I levered the window open. It was surprisingly easy, as if the hinges were oiled.

The way was open. There was then the problem of what to do with the gun, for I would have to jump to catch the ledge and the instrument was too heavy and much too long to carry in the clothes, unless I stuffed it down my leg, in which case I couldn't bend my leg to jump up.

I broke it, unloaded the cartridges, put them in my pocket, then tossed the gun up through the opening. It made a noise and I waited, but nothing happened.

One last look round the museum, and then I sprang up and caught the ledge with my hands. Useful practice at the firm's gym made the rest comparatively easy. I raised myself steadily until I toppled the upper part of my body headfirst into the opening.

The execution was first class. The only trouble was that as I landed face down in the dirt and darkness of the secret way, I felt something press the back of my neck and pin my face to the boards.

It was a foot.

CHAPTER TEN

1

When one is taken by surprise, face down on the floor with a heavy foot pinning you down by the back of the neck, the natural reaction is to try and get the foot off. That is wrong.

The pinner is putting most weight in the leg which pins you down and easing the load on the one he is actually standing on.

In the gloom I could see the stalk of that leg near my shoulder as I lay. I grabbed the ankles and pulled. The leg gave. Instantly the other foot was taken from my neck. I saw both do an evasive dance like a very agile boxer, and then turn and run off into the darkness.

I rolled over and sat up.

The sound of the running was soft, meaning both soft shoes and a very agile, light running person. I got up and took my .38 from my pocket, leaving the shotgun on the floor unloaded.

I was in a tunnel of darkness but at the far

end I could see a square of grey light, which must have been the entrance to it from the outside wall of the house.

There was no running figure in between that light and me, and I made sure there was no one behind me by closing the window and using the small bolt it had to fix it.

My feeling was that something was heading for a crisis. Congle was dead, and more than anything that seemed to point to the fact that nearly the end of this invisible game had been reached.

Congle had been a prime mover in the case of Tregarrok before this, and his release from the charge against him by the jury's belief he had always been too drunk to commit such a clever crime held no water for me.

I knew too well that sober or full of drink, nothing impaired that greedy, ratlike soul from following its own advantage. The story of the London gang he had spread in jail might be true, but also it might be a fabrication, the benefits of which only Congle had been able to appreciate.

There might have been a gang, but it seemed an extraordinarily slow one in making the best of finding Kraw's secret bank boxes. In fact, I believed that the story had been hawked round and carefully considered by gangs.

But for some reason it had been abandoned.

Creeping along in the dark cleared my head, and it seemed to me then a case of Congle spreading a tale to be investigated because, for some reason, he had known it would not be followed up.

Not by the gangs, anyhow. His return to his office might have meant he would rest there awhile, and then at his own convenience, walked in and completed his search for the loot.

But my calling at his office had meant no rest for him. It was possible, too, that hearing me arrive made him think I was not alone, and that the police might be standing off.

He could smell a rat. He had been a rat himself.

His sensible action would then have been to ignore the whole affair for a long while, sit in his office and let us all get bored, give up and go away.

Instead something had shaken him out of that sensible inaction and caused him to go to Tregarrok and take all the risks which that involved.

The risk which in the end had proved too much and now there was no more Congle.

But of whom had he been frightened? Not me. He knew me. If he feared I would find the loot, all he had to do was sigh and work for an honest living and remain a free man.

Or wait, as I say, until I went away. He was the one person who would know I wasn't interested in loot, but only in who was after it.

Therefore he and I should have been

interested in the same thing but we weren't. Why not?

This person hiding in the dark ahead of me perhaps. The quick agile stunt man, Percy?

I stopped and listened. There was a slight movement of air in the passage from the open end and it made a soft shiffing noise on a lot of dead leaves which had drifted in there and stayed to get drier. The faint noise disturbed my hearing for it came from several different places in the tunnel.

The use of a light in such circumstances is never sound, because it is such a good target and give-away, but there seemed no other way of finding the runaway, and I needed to find him before he found me.

I heard nothing but the shifting leaves.

One side or the other of the tunnel there had to be an opening but as the walls were framed in timber like an old ship, it was impossible to tell where one might be without a light.

It was necessary not to pass such an opening and leave my opponent at my back. I brought my tiny pea lamp from my pocket. It had no power for ordinary purposes but just enough to show up an opening, I hoped.

I held it out in my outstretched hand as far from my body as I could, while keeping the pistol in my right hand. I slid the safety catch off on the gun, then turned on the tiny light.

A few seconds passed, very long ones, during

which I was ready to fire at the slightest movement or sound of it, but nothing happened at all.

The runaway had gone into whatever secret room there was. I went on, taking great care to note every sound, but apart from the shifting leaves, there was nothing.

I came to an opening on the left. There was no door. After one last look up and down the tunnel I went through the opening.

From what I could see by the tiny light, it was a small room of very strange shape, doubtless because it had to fit in behind the walls of other rooms without being suspected.

There was an old table and a form by it and both were free of dust. There were some old wooden brass-bound boxes stacked against a timber wall, but there was no sign of any person.

I went round the angles and crannies of the walls and came to an opening with a wooden trap door in it. The catch was not on and I lifted the flap a little.

There was the grey moonlight and a tree close to the opening while below it was the top of the garden wall jutting out from the house by which I had left the women.

By a look round the rest of the room I made sure nobody was hiding, then I went back and opened one of the old boxes.

The tiny light burst into a thousand others as it shone on a collection of jewellery rarely seen just tumbled into a box.

I closed the box and went back to the trapdoor. By opening it further than before I could see the outside of the garden wall where I had left the women.

They weren't there.

I went back to the table and sat on it and turned my light out. There was no need to go through the other boxes; they might be full, or they might not. From what I had seen in the first box there was enough to keep somebody for life even on a black market. Any more would be superfluous.

Unless they were fakes.

The box in the farmhouse chimney, carefully hidden and all traces of the hiding carefully cleaned off. Such care for a box of fakes.

Poxon knew they were fakes because Poxon's father had been a jeweller. So Poxon would know a fake. And having been a student of jewellery she would also have known that the majority of people do not know a fake.

It was Poxon who had said the farmhouse jewels were fakes, when no one else there was in a position to know if they were or not.

The point that bothered me was that there was no reason at all for so carefully hiding a box of stumers, but there was for hiding a box of the real stuff.

Which made it appear that the jewels had been real, but that Poxon didn't want us to think that.

That might mean that she was in partnership with whoever the amateur sweep had been—unless she had hidden the box herself.

There are only two reasons for fake jewellery; to satisfy vanity, or to replace a real object, and in both cases the object is to deceive.

But there is no obvious reason for anyone to make a vast collection of fakes and then hide them.

Because of this I decided the jewels might be real and those in the farmhouse chimney certainly were because their reality was the reason why Congle was dead and also the man at the old farm.

It was then reasonable to think that Congle was still looking for the stones when he was killed.

In which case then the farm worker had been shot for the same reason. He must have known about jewellery hidden in a flue but had chosen the wrong farmhouse to explore.

But then, most people, thinking of a hiding place, would surely choose a ruined and deserted house rather than an occupied one, where the box might be found by the residents.

So the man had chosen the deserted house and been found at it. Or perhaps he had been expected there. Congle had been a great spreader of stories useful to himself, and as I knew, he had tried to shoot that man before. Therefore he had dropped the story of loot being hidden and then followed the dupe and shot him at a favourable moment.

Congle had not been a nice man at all.

Killing that man got rid of a competitor as well as an enemy.

Congle had then thought the time ripe to end his search of Tregarrok for good, but he had thought the boat on the gates an accident, which was what everybody else had thought.

But in fact it gave Poxon and her sister the excuse to be here and give them time to search the building at leisure.

Yet the boat had been there some time, so it was possible that something had happened to make them rush to Tregarrok so fast that they did not meet in time to get a story agreed.

So probably they had come from different directions and only met here. So they had come in a hurry and something had started it.

I thought that reason must be me. I felt sure it was the reason for Congle's being at Tregarrok, but then I had called on his office. How did the Fairlane sisters know I had arrived?

If I'd known then about Zeiss calling on John Marsh, I might have guessed.

With my light I looked into another couple of boxes. There were only a few assorted pieces of jewellery in them, unlike the overflowing first one I had opened.

As I looked I wondered if this whole business had been not so much to do with jewels as with something else, something much more fundamental.

But then the jewels were there as well only I felt there were too many of them.

I went back to the top box and took out a big brooch with gold settings. The hallmark was in position on the back.

I took another piece, an earring, gold set.

There was no hallmark, and a hallmark was the only way I could tell whether a piece was really fake or not. Seven more pieces, chosen at random, had no marks. One after that had.

Mostly fakes, but some real. It must be some kind of a bait. I could think of nothing else, but it started a lot of much better thoughts for me.

2

I got out at the trapdoor and lowered myself down on to the top of the garden wall. The moon seemed brighter, as if the cloud layer was thinning. It was bright enough for me to see that there was no one about on either side of the wall.

I dropped down to the long grass on the inside and looked towards the great door of the house. Everything was quiet, but the door was half open.

My feeling was that all four women were inside, both the Fairlane sisters...

'—my father was a jeweller—'

And Isaac Kraw had been a diamond merchant. I had not taken much account of the

Kraw story because it had merely provided a reason why treasure might be in Tregarrok.

But the discovery of such a lot of it up in that secret room clicked it into place, and Poxon too. Kraw. Kraw might have been her father or he might not, but I thought she had known him and his business and if not his daughter, had worked for him.

A boatyard on the Sussex coast could be of inestimable value to a gentleman dealing genuinely, and then illicitly, with diamonds and other matters.

I was then not too determined to fix on that explanation because all along I had been suspicious of Poxon in one way and another and might be prejudiced against her.

And there was the odd difference of the story that the sisters shared; yes, they both said they had a boatyard, but one said it was at Mar and the other at Shoreham, a difference of two hundred miles plus.

But then they had to stick to the boatyard because of the boat on the gates which they had come to salvage.

As I went slowly and watchfully towards that half open door, I felt I had my theory right and yet I was uneasy. Two items bothered me, almost made me feel I was being followed.

What had Percy come for? Haigh was in some degree in with Congle, for he had acted perfectly when I had called, knowing Congle was in the next room. No, 'I'll see if he's in' but a pretence that he was nowhere near. He might just have been an aide, helping Congle for whatever he could get out of it.

But Percy...

He made no more sense than the box of jewels hidden in the farmhouse chimney.

Jewels hidden in the flue and then everything made clean, shipshape and Bristol fashion.

Jewels in the secret room overflowing from boxes—

A film stunt man wandering about with no apparent purpose...

Films. Of course, films. Where else could you get overflowing boxfuls of sparkling jewellery but in the props room of a film studio?

What better hiding place for real gems than amongst a mass of fakes, so that only an expert would tell which from which, but a thief couldn't?

I stood undecided as to which I should do first; go back to the farmhouse and wait for the person who would certainly come and collect the real stuff in the flue; or go into the mansion first and find the women.

Everything was quiet. I could hear the sea murmuring on the shore, but otherwise it was a still, almost heavy night.

I went across the grass and in at the half open door, stepping to one side of it as soon as I was in. I waited. Nothing broke the silence. I felt that the three women had either gone, or not even come into the house.

A feeling came upon me that someone was there in the darkness and holding quite still, but I could see no shadows that indicated anyone hiding in that gloomy place.

Then I remembered the human spider, the man on the outside wall, and the man up at the fake window leading to the secret room and I moved away from the wall very quickly and looked up into the roof beams.

I saw him standing on one, crouched as if to jump on me and I had moved just in time.

'Take it easy, Percy,' I said. 'I've got a gun on you and I am a competition shot. I won't miss if you jump without my permission.'

I heard him sigh.

'Come on down,' I said. 'Drop on to the big table.'

He dropped easily on to the big central refectory table almost without a sound, then, watching me carefully, he sat down on it.

'Are you waiting for anybody?' I said.

'No.' He shook his head. 'Nobody's coming. The trap was blown. The big boys decided it wasn't worth the risk, not with police blocking off the countryside all round.'

'How did you know?'

'Well, there was this fellow Zeiss and he blew the gaff to some partner of yours and in return he got sea passage in a private boat.

'Only the boat belonged to Kraw's daughters—you've heard of Kraw?'

'Yes.'

'Well, naturally, these girls were interested in Zeiss, not only in him and the loot, but also in a man called Congle. Congle was a man who opened his mouth when it suited him. Congle talking in the right quarters was the reason Kraw was sunk in a load of concrete, and Zeiss knew all that. It tied up with a place—this place.'

'But their excuse for coming was the boat stuck on the gates?'

'Sure. A bit dramatic, even for a film man like me, but it served.'

'So they meant to come and look for father's wicked profits?'

'Sure, sure. And when they found from Zeiss that this was Congle's hometown and he'd recently been let loose again, why it was like a bonus for them.'

'You know them?'

'We filmed some stunts off Brighton for a TV series. They provided boats, I jumped from one to the other at forty knots in a fog—you know the type of thing. In my job you get to know all sorts of people.'

'And so you get all sorts of jobs?'

'All sorts,' he said. 'I'm a soldier of fortune, anybody's buy.' He laughed.

'And what was the point of the trick of throwing yourself over the cliff?'

'That was unfortunate. My sense of humour. I just couldn't resist it. But I hadn't dropped the line, then, so it didn't matter.'

'A line down to the beach?'

'Yes. So they could get to their boat—listen! That's her. Nice engines. They won't stop this side of Spain, you take it from me.'

We heard the soft sound of powerful engines pulling away from somewhere below the cliffs.

'Patrol boats might get in its way and bring them back. Why didn't we hear it arrive? It wasn't down there before dark.'

'We pulled it with a line from up the coast a bit. You know the man on guard outside the farm? He towed it. I told him to see nobody looked over the cliff and we tried to keep you in there so's to be sure, only the silly sod stood the wrong side of the house.'

'Who got those jewellery boxes up in the loft place?'

'I got those for them. It was a bait, you see. For Congle.'

'It was a deliberate plot to murder him, then, and not treasure hunting?'

'That was the object and it's been done. I think you found the murderer just when she was coming away from the job. Bit of a nerve to go back there with you.'

'And to lead me to it.'

'Well, they're a jokey pair.'

'Strange word for it. But the ploy let her slip away, so it had its uses.'

'Well, that's my job done, anyway,' he said. 'Of course I get payment in advance for these jobs. I don't do them just for the fun.'

'You are an accessory to a murder.'

'People like Congle don't count,' he said calmly. 'It's doing good to society, giving him the chop.'

I couldn't disagree with that but didn't say so. Anyway, I was sure Congle had shot his own ex-labourer at the old farm.

'Tell me,' I said, 'did those women find what they came to look for?'

'I'm not sure,' he said. 'You see, they've gone earlier than expected because you'd got too close to what was going on. They knew you were suspicious.'

'They should have agreed a story before they came here.'

I told him about the different placings of their boatyard.

'Perhaps your Poxon didn't want to make it a long acquaintance,' he said, 'so it wouldn't have mattered. I think she was shattered when you saw her sister out on the cliff. It was careless of her, and damned silly to think she hadn't been seen by you, of all people. I suppose then she just had to tell as much of the truth as there was on the spur of the moment.'

'Is that boat on the gates theirs?'

'It was. It's mine now.' He dug under his jersey and brought out some folded papers from his shirt pocket. 'The docs, my friend, the proof of ownership. Part of my perks, and I may say not too much, considering I have to wear these special toes on my shoes to get me up walls. You should have seen me in "Gorgon the Terrible"; right up to the top of the castle wall—and then fell bloody off because the wall gave way. Of course, I got compensation ...' He stuffed the papers back. 'You don't mind if I go now? I want to take Laura back to town. I promised.'

'I'm not the police,' I said. 'But what about the boat?'

'I shall sell the TV film rights of that. "How to get a boat off spiked railings, using fork lift trucks, cranes etcetera". Should be a hit on Children's Hour. They'll pay all the costs, you see.'

He went off. Using my small lamp I looked in the places I knew in the house and specially the place where the original loot had been found months before, but it did not look as if anyone had been there.

The fake jewels had been planted as a mislead, while the real ones had been stacked in the farmhouse flue, that seemed sure.

I went back to the farmhouse. Only Freddie was there. She said Laura had gone with Percy. She got some supper while I got the box out of the flue and put it on the table. The jewels were still in it.

'Well?' she said, looking at it.

'I think somebody will come and pick it up.'

'Oh,' she said, and poured some home made

beer. 'When?'

'It must be tonight. The police are bound to look round Tregarrok in the morning, just to make sure all is well and they'll find Congle, so then they'll ask questions etcetera.' I had caught the ad lib from Percy.

'Yes, I see,' she said. 'Well, wouldn't it be best to shove it back in the chimney? Then whoever it is will come in and you'll be able to make the snatch.'

'Maybe.' I put it back.

'I was wondering,' she said. 'It might really belong to Poxon and her sister. I mean, their father was a jewel man.'

'It's possible, but they went without it.'

'Well, they were in rather a rush. And they didn't seem to be very hard up.'

We put the light out and sat there waiting. The dogs were told to be quiet and stayed under the table, content.

The dawn came up. She got some tea. She was calm, almost unconcerned, and into my mind came a certain thought.

'Of course it was Poxon who put it up there,' she said. 'And so she'll be back. And so, leave it. Say nothing until she does come back.'

'Is that what you really want me to do?'

'Well, what's the good of keeping on stirring things up? What good will it do to give the box to the police? Nobody's ever going to claim it. And you said there was no list of jewellery reported stolen, so whoever it was stolen from shouldn't have had it anyway.' She shrugged. 'It all seems so pointless trying to find justice in a barrelful of crooks.'

'I see what you mean.'

'If anything does happen I can let you know.'

'Of course.'

So I left it and she didn't let me know. I was not really surprised. The trouble with a spell of being in love is that one's normal perspicacity is blunted.

Yet one still makes rather special allowances, provided nobody will suffer from it.

What am I moralising about? I could have been quite wrong.

We hope you have enjoyed this Large Print book. Other Chivers Press or G.K. Hall & Co. Large Print books are available at your library or directly from the publishers.

For more information about current and forthcoming titles, please call or write, without obligation, to:

Chivers Press Limited
Windsor Bridge Road
Bath BA2 3AX
England
Tel. (01225) 335336

OR

G.K. Hall & Co.
P.O. Box 159
Thorndike, Maine 04986
USA
Tel. (800) 223–2336

All our Large Print titles are designed for easy reading, and all our books are made to last.